HarperCollins *Children's Books*

First published in Great Britain by HarperCollins *Children's Books* in 2009
HarperCollins *Children's Books* is a division of HarperCollins*Publishers* Ltd
77-85 Fulham Palace Road, Hammersmith, London W6 8JB

www.harpercollins.co.uk

1

ISBN: 978-0-00-728359 0

Printed and bound in England by
Clays Ltd, St Ives plc

For Alex

(and Reg)

One (Sam)

I saw a girl. Just a kid. It's not what happened first, but it's a good place to start. I can see her now. She could be standing right in front of me. I wish she was.

Dark red hair, cream white skin, eyes to the ground.

I was walking past and she was there in a doorway, an open doorway on to the street. Behind her was another door into the place, a bar I think, or a club maybe. And around her, between the two doorways, was just black, pure matt black. Her clothes were black, so her dark red hair and her pale face and hands were the only places of light.

She looked like she was appearing out of the night, sitting for a painter who'd been dead two hundred years. I'm not joking. There she was, in the rougher end of Camden High Street, looking like she belonged on the wall of the National Gallery.

I kept walking and I held her picture in my head, and I remember thinking, *What if I went back and said hello?* What if I told her how she looked, and how much I wished I had a camera and some idea of how to use it? I'd scare her, a big bloke like me. She'd think I was a freak. She'd move away and leave her place of perfect darkness and ruin the picture forever.

So I didn't. I marked her down as one out of the eight hundred mental snapshots I'd taken that minute. It's what you do in a place so crammed full of things to look at. Blink and keep moving. I'd been here less than one day, and even I'd been in London long enough to know that.

My name is Sam and I'm not from here.

I grew up in a house beneath a mountain, hidden in a dip that filled with snow in the winter, with water in the spring. Night time there was proper darkness, a total absence of light, apart from the stars which were infinite and spread just right to show you the curved shape of the sky.

There aren't any stars in the city. I used to drag my mattress over to the window and lie on my back looking out at the damp blanket of orange that bounced off every available surface, at the flashing wings of aeroplanes.

The day I left home was like this: high sky, still air, shouting birds. I woke up and it was beautiful, and I hated the sight of it because there was no way I could stay. I forced myself to lie in bed until Dad had gone, staring at the sun through my window for so long that I could see it with my eyes shut.

I was sitting at my desk, dressed and ready to go when Mum banged on my door around eight. Three short raps. She made the distance beween us obvious even in the way she did that.

Afterwards I often wondered how things would have been different if she'd known I was leaving, if she'd have kept those feelings to herself just that once. But you can't go around treating everyone like you might never see them again, just in case. And anyway, it was way too late by then. I already knew how she felt.

Missing the bus was way easier than catching it. I changed my school sweatshirt in the broken down barn at the end of our lane and stashed it in my bag. And then I hitched into town to catch the train. Aaron Hughes the old farmer picked me up – truck like the inside of a haystack, trousers held up with bailer twine, vicious Jack Russell on the passenger seat; that kind of old. He drove at about ten miles an hour, which is not exactly getaway speed. But he didn't hear too well and he wasn't bothered about talking, and I was glad about that. I wondered what he would do if he knew he was helping me escape.

The sky was this intense blue, palest at the bottom, dark

around the edges. The surface of the hills shifted with the light, darkened with the shadows of high clouds. I was sick to death of all of it: the same curves, the same trees, the same beauty. But because I knew it was the last time, I stared like I'd never seen it before.

Aaron laughed. He said something about the land being like a woman, stunning when you leave her and grey and ordinary when you don't.

We were quiet then. I didn't know what to say to that.

The station was about a twenty minute walk from where he dropped me. People were waiting on the platform, saying goodbye to each other, huddling around cars. I didn't see anyone I knew, thank God. I bought a ticket, crossed the iron bridge over the railway and sat there in the tunnelling wind on my own.

This is what I remember of the train journey. Identical twins. Women with shining scruffy black hair sleeping against each other two tables away. They were thin and tired, and they kept opening their eyes and not speaking, and then closing them again. Each of them was beautiful because there were two of her, like someone put a mirror down the middle of the train.

A group of kids behind me on their way to a maths

marathon. They spoke so everyone could hear, like they were important, like nothing could touch them, like being good at maths was all you'd ever need to make sense of the world. I wanted to set them straight, but I knew they'd find out soon enough without me.

A little boy at the window of another train, crammed in, surrounded by arms, the sleeve of a quilted jacket squashed flat against the glass like someone pulling a face.

I took the sim card out of my phone, dropped it in a half empty paper teacup and gave it a stir. The woman opposite me stared without blinking while I did it and then went back to her magazine. I made sure I still had my money on me. I'd been taking some out of the bank every day. I kept checking it was there, all the time, because it was all I had.

The mountains shrank and the land flattened out, got boxed in and carved up. The view from the window was cramped and ordinary and fascinatingly strange. The twins woke up and looked out at it without saying a word.

I closed my eyes.

The first thing I learned about London was not to smile. I got off the train and looked around. The platform emptied like an organised stampede. I smiled at this man in a suit, dark-skinned, middle-aged, clean-shaven. He was walking towards me. The shine on his shoes reflected the sky through the glass roof of the station. I smiled and it didn't go down so well. He did three things, lightning quick, in less than a second. I watched him. He changed the rhythm of his walk ever so slightly. He looked hard at me, like steel, to make sure he wasn't seeing things. Then he let his eyes cloud over, so he was still looking, but right through me, never at me. The one thing he definitely didn't do was smile back. I learned pretty quick that the only people who smile at everyone in London are newcomers and the clinically insane.

Later, in the ticket hall at Paddington, I saw more people in one go than I'd seen in the whole of my life before. Thousands lining up for tickets and funnelling through turnstiles, going up escalators and coming down. I stood dead still at the eye of the storm, just one of me, and stared. I kept looking at this list I'd scribbled on the back of an envelope, like it might help. I couldn't read my own writing.

Everyone else knew where to go and moved in swift, strong lines that picked me up and took me in the wrong direction, like the river at home after a night of rain.

I thought about Max then. He came back to me in the middle of all that sound and rhythm and colour and fume-smell and movement. He surprised me. I thought about walking behind him in the dappled darkness of the woods.

I pictured his permanent frown, his sticking out ears, his chaotic hair. I thought about the nervous flicker of his smile.

It was all I could do to keep breathing.

You know when people say they wish the floor would open up and swallow them whole? Well, it's pretty easily done, if you really mean it. I came out of Camden Town Station at twenty-nine minutes past four and vanished without a trace. Nobody knew who I was. I couldn't stop smiling.

The sky was lower than I was used to. I went into a baker's and bought a sandwich, and I couldn't understand half of what the girl behind the counter said to me because she said it all so fast. I took too long counting out the right money and I could hear her foot tapping and she didn't smile back, in fact she didn't even look at me. The sandwich tasted of nothing and made me incredibly thirsty. I bought a Coke from a paper shop that you couldn't fit more than two bodies in at one time. It was so crammed full of things to buy they forgot to leave room for people.

That's what Camden looked like to me – it was the first thing I noticed. There was stuff for sale everywhere and I wondered who the hell would want to buy any of it.

I sat down on the wall of a bridge over the canal and finished my drink. I opened my bag and looked inside, for no reason at all. It was so loud. Layers of noise crowded and collided in my head, like sheep in a lorry, and made it hard to think. I walked all the way down one side of the street, into the yards, stopping for everything, studying everything, and then all the way back down the other. It was dirty, all greys instead of greens, like everything had a coat of dust on it. I felt like I needed to wash my hands even though I'd hardly touched anything.

I read about the dust on the London Underground once, that there's tonnes of it every week and it's mostly human skin. I hadn't really believed it. But now I wondered if that was what was covering everything – pieces of all the people I'd already seen and all the people I hadn't.

That's when I saw the kid in the doorway, when I was walking up and down thinking about the dust. That's when I filed her away in my memory box of people you don't ever speak to. I was killing time because I had no idea what should happen next. It's probably why I noticed her.

I went into a pub and had a pint. The man behind the bar didn't look at me, didn't ask how old I was. Nobody looked at me. It was like magic, like finding an invisible cloak.

It was the opposite of home.

It's what I'd longed for, for weeks and weeks, to be the blind spot in a room, the black hole in the universe, to be absent without trying to at all.

I wanted to stay like that forever.

Later, I stood on the pavement outside the pub and tried to make sense of where I was. I remember pretending the road was a river, fed by other smaller roads like the streams that run off the hills, but thick with cars and bikes and buses instead of water. I remember thinking I'd had too much to drink.

Across the street a black plastic sign with pink writing said *The Kyprianos Hotel*. There was a fracture in the plastic and a round hole, like someone had thrown a tennis ball in there, or a rock. I had my hand around all the money in my pocket. I could afford it, I knew that, maybe not for long, but I suddenly needed to sleep.

I'd never stayed in a hotel before. It didn't amount to much, apart from some soap in a box and a plastic shower cap, and a bathroom where you had to practically stand on the loo seat if you wanted to close the door. I didn't close the door because there was nobody watching. I was completely and utterly on my own.

I almost regretted it then. I very nearly decided I'd done the wrong thing. But I swerved away from it at the last minute and kept my eyes on the road.

If only I'd learned to do that earlier.

I couldn't sleep because there was too much going on outside the window – a whole orchestra of sirens and yelling and footsteps and door slams and engines. I wondered how anyone ever slept. I stared at a clamshell stain in one corner of the ceiling and thought about becoming someone new with nothing to be ashamed of, no past, just a future.

I thought about how weird it was, to be missing in one place while you're right there in another.

Two (Bohemia)

I was waiting for my mum. That's what I was doing. I was pressing patterns into a piece of old chewing gum with the bottom of my shoe. There were more than nineteen pieces of gum on the square of pavement outside the bar. I was counting them.

I wasn't allowed in cos I'm underage. That's why I was waiting outside in the black doorway in the freezing cold. She was in there for ages. Mr Thing and her weren't friends any more, which meant she'd also lost her job and we had to leave the flat. Things happen that way a lot because Mum's good at putting all of her eggs in one boyfriend.

We went so she could collect her wages and they had one more massive row while I stood outside counting spat out gum, trying not to listen. When she stormed out her mascara had slipped and the end of her nose was red, and she was halfway through a sentence about what a something he was.

When she saw me she rubbed her nose with the back of her hand and cracked a smile. She's got nice teeth, my mum, all straight and small. Not like my mouth, which is still full of holes and frilly edges, even though I'm ten already. I hope I get teeth like her when I'm finished. I hope I hurry up.

"Let's go," Mum's pretty teeth said. "Let's spend some of his money, quick."

She got me by the hand and we walked really fast across the road, and I thought she was saying stuff to me that I couldn't hear.

"What?" I said, and she turned to me and I saw she had her mobile out already.

We packed before we went to see Mr Thing cos Mum'd been expecting it and she'd helped herself to a few extras out of his house, like towels and wine and stuff. We'd stashed our bags in a pub.

She phoned around and found a place, quick as a flash. She's clever like that.

"Small apparently," she said, and then licked her lips. "Like we could afford anything else".

We lugged everything from the pub and stood outside the house with our suitcases. I looked at Mum, her big black glasses reflecting the sun, a little smudge of lipstick on her teeth when she smiled. I didn't have time to point it out cos she rang a couple of bells and this lizard man in a pair of faded jeans appeared in the basement.

He stood there talking to her. I *swear* he was trying to see up her skirt. I tried to tell her, to pull her a bit out of the way, but she just said, "Not now!" sort of through her grin, so I glared at him instead. He was the landlord and I didn't like him at first, smarmy old scale-face called Steve.

The corridor smelled funny, of cabbage and pot noodle and then something else like bleach with flowers in it. There was a big stack of old letters so the door couldn't open all the way. Steve kicked it to one side with his *cowboy* boot and it fanned out over the floor. The carpet was the colour of a camel and looked like a camel had been eating it. He said it needed to be "refurbished" and when he said the word, he flowered his arms around like we might see it change before our very eyes, but we didn't. There was a bike against the wall, with no front tyre and no saddle. It made me think of dinosaur bones in the desert. It was locked to the radiator with a big big chain.

"That's Mick's," he said. "He lives below you. The rest of it is in his kitchen."

We were on our way upstairs when an old lady came through the front door. It was only me that turned round to see. Her little dog started sniffing around all the envelopes and lifted its leg for a pee. It made me laugh, the sound of it landing. I didn't tell. The old lady winked at me and tickled the dog and jingled her keys and went into her flat.

Our house was at the top. Steve carried one of Mum's bags and she took one of mine. I dragged the other one up with two hands cos it was easier than lifting and it made this sound, scratch-thump, scratch-thump, on every step.

There was a loo, straight ahead, like as soon as you walked in, actually a bathroom, a kitchen to the left and a room with a sofa bed in it. I like sofa beds cos they're a secret and you can have a bedroom any time you want, night or day. This one was a weird peachy colour that wasn't so nice, but I didn't mind cos it was bigger than our old one and it didn't have such sharp corners.

"What do you think, Mum?" I said. "It's all right, isn't it?"

She frowned at me for calling her Mum in public and then she said to Steve, "We'll take it."

They shook hands and she did that laugh she does for boys only, which sounds like tiny stones landing on the high bit of a piano.

After she handed over the money and Steve handed over

the key and left, she did a bit of ranting. That's what I call it when she's angry and she talks like she's forgotten I'm there or I could be anyone, or something.

She said that maybe this was what Steve meant by "furnished" – one crap sofa, rubbish in the bins, not even a table, a couple of plates – but she could think of another name for it. She couldn't believe how low she'd sunk. She said the place was filthy. She said, how did we know he wasn't just re-letting to us while the people who really lived there were out at work?

"Huh!" she said, like a cross sort of laughing. "Imagine them coming home to you and me."

While she ranted I did our Mary Poppins trick. I call it that cos there's a bit I really like in the film where Mary has a bag made out of carpet and it's full of stuff you'd never fit in a bag in real life, lamps and flowerpots and everything. My bag is a bit like that. Unpacking it never seems to end and there's all sorts of stuff you can fling about until it feels more like home. Me and Mum's favourite thing in that bag was a fold-up cardboard star with holes cut out. It was white when we got it and I painted it ages ago, when I was like six, and even though I didn't do such a great job of it I never let her throw it away. It goes over the light bulb in your ceiling and makes everything look like a disco at Christmas.

Except there wasn't a light bulb, just an empty socket hanging, so I said I'd go to the shop and get one.

Mum was in the bathroom by then. I know what she does in there.

The street was way nicer than where Mr Thing lived, which was just flats and more flats and dark places I didn't like being in by myself. For a start it was quiet, except for the cars whizzing across at the end. There was a garden on the other side of the road and a pub halfway down. The pub was covered in green tiles, like a bathroom. The houses were all the same and sort of elegant. I walked slowly, looking into all the windows. You can learn a lot about a place that way, about who lives there and the kind of stuff they keep. Like in some places there's always books, more than you need really, and some houses look like they're actually in a magazine, with the right flowers and everything. And some have net curtains older than me and Mum put together, and you can't see in at all, but you can see they need washing and that nobody who lives in them ever goes out.

In our new street it was harder to see cos the bottom windows were under the pavement and the next windows up were too high. The basements mostly had leaves and bicycles and dustbins and broken chairs in, apart from one that had little trees cut to look like squirrels, but you couldn't swing a cat down there.

Each house was cut up into so many flats you wondered where they put them. I read the little lit-up cards by the door on my way back in to ours and tried to work them out.

Basement was **S Robbins**, which was lizard-face Steve.

Flat one said **Davy**, the old lady with the peeing dog.

Flat two was water damaged, all brown and cloudy so I couldn't read it.

Flat three said **Flat three**, which seemed pointless and was where the rest of the bike was.

Four was ours now, but it still said **Fatnani**.

The first thing I did, before the light bulb even, was cut a little piece of paper the right size off an envelope. I wrote **CHERRY & BOHEMIA**, drew some stars and fireworks, to put downstairs at the button for number four.

Cherry's my mum's name. I'm supposed to call it her now I'm ten cos the word MUM makes her feel old. Cherry loves it the times someone asks if we're sisters. She knows they don't mean it and they know she doesn't believe them, but everyone plays along anyway. That's what she told me. She said, "The men I hang out with are suckers."

The time I like her best is some Sunday afternoons. We stay in our pyjamas, watch TV if we've got one, and eat what we want under a duvet. Some Sundays, she looks at me like she hasn't seen me all week.

Steve the landlord lent us a broom and some bin bags and we cleaned up. Mum sprayed some perfume about so the whole flat smelled of her. When he came to get his stuff back, he asked Mum if she wanted to come out for a drink, just down the road at the pub that looked like a bathroom.

"You can come if you want, little lady," he said to me. "Have a lemonade and a packet of crisps."

Mum said I was all right here. She said, "You don't mind do you, Bo, if I pop out?"

It was fine with me. I like being in a new place because there's loads to do and look at and think about, and it takes longer than normal to mind being on your own. Mum gave me a pound for some chips if I got hungry and she said she wouldn't be long. I put the money in my pocket and I made the sofa into a bed for later. I unpacked my clothes and made two really neat piles of them under the window. Then I played snake on Mum's phone and made a few calls – not real ones because if she ran out of money I'd be in for it, and anyway, who would I speak to? I pretended to be like her when she's on it, talking really quiet and biting her nails and saying things like "No way" and "ten minutes" and "you out tonight or what?"

Before she left I showed her the card I made for the front door. She liked it. She said she'd take it with her and put it by our bell. Maybe nobody would notice. But at least it showed we were alive in there.

Three (Sam)

It happened faster than I'd thought, my new life getting started. First I found a job, stacking shelves in an all night sort of supermarket. I only went in for a carton of milk.

From the shelves I stacked most, I'd say most people went in for SuperTenants and five-litre bottles of cider. The hours were strange and peopled with drunks. I kept my head down. Nobody asked me any awkward questions and they didn't need any paperwork, and they were as content as I was not to bother being friends.

And I found somewhere to live.

My place at number 33 Georgiana Street was the third bell of five. All the other bells had a name on apart from mine, and no name suited me fine. I found it outside a newsagent's on a notice board. A guy came out while I was standing there and stuck a postcard on with a pin. I watched him walk back in the shop before I read it.

I'd been throwing my money away at the hotel for nearly a week. I couldn't afford it and I couldn't go home. I didn't want to be one of those people who moves to London and then ends up sleeping on the streets before they know it. The postcard said STUDIO FLAT. NICE VIEWS. CHEAP RENT. NO DSS. 2 MINS TUBE. DEPOSIT.

I phoned the number from a call box that stank so hard I had to keep the door open with my leg. I was standing at the end of my new road.

The landlord's name was Steve. He lived in the basement. His skin was the exact dead texture of his leather jacket. He did the welcome tour, meaning the communal bathroom and the under-stairs cupboard where my meter was, and I couldn't take my eyes off the folds and creases in his cheeks.

The electricity was pay as you go, same as the rent, which Steve kept telling me was way below the going rate, and which had to be cash in a brown envelope, I'm guessing so he could stuff it under his mattress and not tell anybody. I handed over half of everything I'd ever saved for the first month's rent. The whole place was pretty trashed, but it felt so good to shut the door to my own room and stand with my back against it. It could have been exactly what I'd dreamed of doing with the money all along.

The place had a little kitchen and a bigger room for everything else, like eating and reading and sitting and thinking and sleeping. The floorboards were painted in thick black gloss with stuff trapped in it, hairs and fluff and sharper lumps, like bugs in amber. There were two massive windows, floor to ceiling, that flooded the place with streetlight all night long and let in the sounds of outside. You are never alone with noise and light, not completely.

From my windows I could see straight into other windows, then across the pattern of rooftops and into the tower of a Greek Orthodox church, and down on to the street below. I spent a long time looking.

It took me about a week to remember where I was when I woke up.

On the first day I cleaned the flat. I found a folded-up note between the floorboards that said *please let me stay in this house forever, please let me, please*. The handwriting was small and spiky and distinctive, all the words joined together like one long word. I closed it up and put it back where I found it, and I felt sorry that whoever wrote it didn't get what they wanted. I felt sorry for them that I was there instead.

When everything was clean I unpacked my bag, which took all of ten seconds. Two T-shirts, three pairs of socks, a spare pair of jeans, toothbrush, toothpaste and soap, a spare jumper, the school uniform I'd taken off, the shell of my phone and two unreadable books which belonged to Max and should have been given back a long time ago.

On the second day I hung blankets on the windows, but they kept falling down so I gave up and learned how to live in a goldfish bowl without caring, like everyone else.

On the third I worked out how to use the little oven. Someone else's cooking burned off the red elements and filled the room with hot, damp smoke.

On the fourth someone upstairs had a domestic in the darker hours of morning. Things kept falling past my windows on to the road below. Clothes float with grace and land silently, while cutlery is more chaotic.

On the fifth the electricity kicked out halfway through my shower because I'd forgotten to charge my top-up key.

On the sixth I walked in on somebody in the communal bathroom. They were just a shadow behind a curtain, but they were shouting.

On the seventh I ate toast and cream of tomato soup for the fourth time that week, and I thought about home and how I could never go back there.

On the eighth day it was raining. I watched the puddles growing on the road. Why did it make me think about me and

Max, staying late at school? I didn't want it to. It was the rain and the books by my bed that did it.

Max was chess club and I was football. I can't play chess and he's rubbish at football. Mum drove him home across the wind battered common which was bedraggled with sheep and rotting bracken. The house stood at a bend in the road, an L-shaped farmhouse with geese and dogs and mud in the yard. It had rained and the road was streaming down the hill towards us, and the windscreen was blind with puddle water.

We walked through his yard to the front door while Mum turned the car around. He didn't knock. We just walked in and left our shoes inside the door. The house was warm and smelt of cinnamon, gold and orange against the grey of outside. I followed him into the kitchen and his mum was there, warming herself like a cat against the Aga.

Max's mum didn't think much of me. "Hello," she said, and Max pretty much ignored her, but I looked at her and smiled because she wasn't my family to ignore. Her hair was wet, bleeding water into the fabric of her shirt like blotting paper.

Max grabbed two apples from the fruit bowl and offered one to me across the table. I shook my head, so he offered it to her and she took it and bit hard. It was quiet between the three of us, and awkward.

"Wait there," Max said suddenly without looking at me. "I'll just get that thing."

I had no idea what he was talking about.

I stayed where I was while he climbed the stairs and walked across the room over our heads. I listened to the wall clock and the hum of the fridge. There was a hole in my sock.

Max's mum didn't talk to me. She finished the apple. She arched her back and stretched her arms above her head. I saw the skin at her hips, above her jeans, below the lift of her shirt. Then she turned her back and filled a saucepan at the sink, started chopping carrots. I wasn't there to her. I might have been a ghost in the room.

I was glad when Max came back with the thing – a book he'd been talking about in the car, something complicated about life on other planets. According to this book, there were so many galaxies and universes out there, even if the odds against life were a billion to one, there'd still be a billion planets teeming with it. As he gave it to me his mum looked at us and laughed quickly to herself. She knew I was never going to read it. I could tell just by the cover that I'd get bogged down on the first page and never pick it up again.

But Max wanted me to leave with something, if not an apple then a book, so I took it. I held its spine and flicked through the pages with my thumb. Mum beeped outside in the yard

and I said I should be going, and Max's mum left the room.

"See you mate," I said, and Max said, "Bye," and she said nothing.

I was putting my shoes back on at the door when he came running out of the kitchen. His socks made a shushing noise on the floorboards.

"Take this one as well," he said. He was out of breath.

"Another book," I said.

"*The Ant Colony*," he said, in a voice like you hear at the cinema. "By Dr Bernard O Hopkins."

I laughed. "Thanks Max."

"It's brilliant," he said, looking at the book and not at me. "A real page turner."

It was so like Max to talk about an ant book like that, like it was a thriller or something.

I said, "I won't be able to put it down."

He nodded, like that was the right answer, and he stood in the orange light of the doorway and watched me walk to the car.

On the drive home Mum and I talked about the books Max had given me. "Ants?" she said. "What a surprise." Because Max was obsessed with them, how organised they were, how many of them there might be, how they all worked together like one animal. Max told me a long time ago that looking down at them made him think he was a giant towering over the earth.

Ants were what we did when we were seven and eight and nine. It was all Max wanted to do. I was like the genius professor's assistant or something. We dug and photographed and measured. We tracked and timed and watched. We collected them in bottles. Max pickled specimens in vinegar and kept them in the garden shed. He'd forget where we were and who I was even, and everything was just about the ants.

When we got older, and everyone wanted to play football and drive cars on the common and get wrecked and show off down the river to girls, Max was still into ants. There wasn't a cure for his ant thing.

I showed Mum the other book. I said, "Do you think the life on other planets idea comes from watching ants?"

"What do you mean?"

"Well, ants are kind of weird, like from outer space, and Max has told me before he thinks humans are just like ants, even less if you put them in the context of the universe."

"Very scientific." Mum was smiling at me. "Some of his brain cells are rubbing off."

"Leave it out, Mum," I said.

She said, "I get vertigo just thinking about life on this planet, never mind scouting around somewhere else for more."

We started inventing intergalactic package holidays, imagining a time when everybody had got bored of space travel because it was too easy, because everyone was doing it, because it was just not cool. I said Max might find someone nearer his IQ on planet Zargon.

Mum said, "What planet is he going to find his people skills on?"

She said this because Max is one of those clever people who are also about the shyest, most awkward you could meet. Often this can be mistaken for just rude.

"He was talking to you," I said to Mum. "That's a start isn't it?"

"When was he talking to me?" she said.

"Today, in the car, about the book."

"No," she said, "he was talking to you."

I smiled at Mum. "He was talking to *you*. He was *looking* at me."

"See?" she said. "People skills. How do you know that anyway?"

"I know Max," I said. "Haven't I known him all my life?"

I told her that in school Max was different, in class anyway. In class Max didn't speak in sentences – he spoke in whole paragraphs.

"Well, not to me he doesn't," Mum said. "I'm lucky if I get one syllable."

I said, "Some people think one syllable is enough. Like Max's Mum. She hardly talks to me."

"Don't get me started on that woman," Mum said. "God knows what she's got against you. I've no idea."

"Whatever," I said, and I looked out of the window at the rain and thought about something else. Like Rosie, this girl at school I was trying to impress. And Mr Hanlan, the Geography teacher who should've been a prison officer, and whether he'd notice I copied Max's homework, and what he would do if he did. And what I was going to eat when I got home because I was starving.

I watched myself in that car, my head leaning against the water-beaded window, my mind on a lot of nothing. I watched from where I was sitting in a room in Camden with black floorboards, and I thought, if you knew when your life was about to start going wrong, would you change it before it was too late?

Four (Bohemia)

The old lady with the dog was called Isabel. She seemed all right to me. Mum told me to watch out cos people like that were never nice for nothing.

I was watching out, but I was just walking past her door when she said, "Come on in, whoever you are."

It was like walking past a phone box when it rings. I've always wanted to do that. And then for the phone call to actually be for me.

She was in the kitchen. She said, "Help me get the lid off this bloody yoghurt. Damn stuff is supposed to be good for you and the stress of it is going to finish me."

She had the pliers out and everything. She'd been trying to pull off the side of the pot cos she couldn't see where the lid started. I flipped it open in about three seconds.

First she looked angry with it and then she laughed.

"I'm Isabel," she said. "I saw your nice door sticker. Is your name Cherry or Bohemia?"

"Bohemia."

"Where did you get a name like that?" she said.

I shrugged. "Most people just call me Bo."

"Well, it's not a piece of fruit at least," she said, sort of under her breath so I wouldn't hear it, except I did. "Cherry your mum's real name, is it?"

"I think so," I said, because I'd never been asked that question before.

"Cherry Chapstick?"

"No, Cherry Hoban," I said.

She started spooning yoghurt into a mug. I was looking at it so she asked me if I wanted some and handed me the rest of the pot. She asked me how old I was and I told her I was ten.

"Why aren't you at school, Bohemia Hoban?" she said.

I liked that she used my whole name. It made me feel like somebody important. I said I was home-schooled cos that's what Mum says.

Isabel put her hands on her hips then and clucked her tongue and said, "What lesson is it now then?"

"Yoghurt opening," I told her, and she laughed.

She said being home-schooled was a lot more than

wandering about the place waiting for my mum to wake up.

"She is awake,' I said, which was actually true.

She said, "If your mum got a whiff of what home-school was about you'd be down the local primary in a second. Home-skiving's what you're doing."

See? That's why Mum didn't like Isabel.

I didn't look at her, even though I know she was looking at me. I ate some more yoghurt before she could ask for it back.

"So you've met us all then," she said.

"I've met you and the landlord with the face."

"That's Steve," she said. "Don't stare. It was an accident with a facial peel."

I asked her what one of those was and then I wished I hadn't because it was something to do with burning your old skin off with acid.

I gave her back the yoghurt. "Why would someone want to do that?" I said.

She told me not to underestimate the power of getting old, or something. "Ask your mum," she said. "Watch her closely when she hits forty."

I asked her who else there was to meet.

"Well, you've got Mick to come – beard, bike, body odour. Met him yet?"

"Nope."

"Aren't you the lucky one." She looked at her ceiling. "The flat above me's empty, but it won't be for long."

"What about your dog?" I said, and I asked her what it was called.

"Doormat," she said. "Where is he?"

I laughed. "Doormat," I said after her. "I don't know where he is, I haven't seen him. Only that time when he was peeing."

"He's always peeing," she said. "He's trying to be macho. Go and have a look in his basket, would you? It's by my bed. You have to boot him out in the mornings sometimes, tell him who's boss."

When I was out of the room she called after me, "I'll make you some toast."

Doormat was curled up in his basket with his face hidden in his bottom. He wagged his tail a bit, just at the tip, and he stretched like everything hurt. I picked him up and took him to the kitchen.

"Don't spoil my dog," Isabel said. "Make him use his legs or I don't know what'll happen."

I put the dog down and he lay in the corner and hid his face in his bottom again. You really couldn't tell which end of him was which, like a dog doughnut.

"What does your mum do for work?" Isabel said. She had her back to me while she cut the bread.

I said she was "between jobs" because I like the way it sounds, all grown up. I said she was having an interview at the pub down the road and she was getting ready for it right now. "She was there last night and the man offered her one, just like that."

"I bet he did. You tell her I can always babysit if she needs."

"I don't need a babysitter. I can sit myself," I said.

"Well, not when you're ten dear, that's not really allowed. But you know where I am."

That's when I told her the rules of babysitting because I found them out once in a library, to be sure. The rules are that you can leave your child at home whenever you like as long as you can get home in fifteen minutes and they are good at looking after themselves and being sensible and they have your phone number somewhere. So seeing as I'm very sensible and the pub was only down the road, I wouldn't be needing a babysitter at all. That's what I told her.

Nobody ever believes me. Isabel didn't believe me either. She scribbled her phone number on a piece of paper and then she made me learn it and say it to her without looking, and then she asked me what I wanted on my toast.

"Anything."

She asked me if I slept well and I said, "Fine, thanks. Me and Mum slept like logs." I crossed my fingers she didn't hear

Mum coming in at four in the morning. I know it was four cos she made so much noise doing it. I think she tripped over and whoever was with her couldn't see well enough in the dark to help her up. I think it was Steve.

I said, "Mum?" And I sat up in bed to see what was going on.

Mum said, "Shush, go to sleep, it's four o'clock in the morning." So that's how I know.

They went into the kitchen and sat on the floor, and Steve must've been a very funny man cos Mum was just laughing and laughing. Maybe he told Mum about his facial peel.

I smiled at Isabel right through my lie, without even blinking, and she smiled back exactly the same, so maybe she knew and maybe she didn't, but neither of us was going to say.

She put a pile of toast on the table. Isabel made her own bread. It had all lumps and bits in it, but it wasn't as bad as it sounds.

I was on about my fifth bit when I heard Mum's shoes on the stairs. She was coming down carefully cos of the heels. I could picture her, sort of sideways and a bit stiff looking, pressing her hands against the walls. I brushed the crumbs off my front and Doormat jumped up and started hoovering them straight away, like a living, breathing dust buster. He followed me when I went and put my head out the door. Maybe he thought I'd leave a trail of crumbs.

"What are you doing in there?" Mum said. She looked pretty and important, and you couldn't tell she'd had two late nights in a row at all.

"Just visiting Isabel."

"Oh yeah?" she said and she came in the flat and almost trod on the dog. "Oh shit!" she said "Sorry, dog," as she walked in the kitchen.

"It's funny cos his name is Doormat," I said to her, but it was only me who was laughing.

"Hello, Isabel," she said and she sounded really loud in the tiny kitchen. "I'm Cherry, Bo's mum. Is she bothering you at all? You all right with her in here?"

"I invited her in," Isabel said. She wasn't really smiling.

"Well, that's nice," Mum said. "I'm off now. Job interview. I'll be back in a bit. Wish me luck."

I put my arms round her waist and she smelled all lovely, and she kissed me in that way she does when she's thinking about her lipstick, all gentle and hardly there, like an eyelash or a butterfly.

Mum was almost out the door when Isabel called after her, asking should she give me my lunch as well as my breakfast. There was a bit of an edge in the way she said it that made me feel bad for eating so much toast.

"No need," Mum said, clicking back in and looking hard

at me. "I'll be back by then. And Bo has lunch money, don't you, darling?"

I shook my head. It was quiet and nobody moved. I counted to three. Then Mum opened her purse and shoved a crumpled fiver in my hand. It was soft and old like tissue. I opened it out to have a proper look. I didn't know what to think. I never normally got that much just for lunch.

Mum told me not to spend it all at once and then she said, "Come and kiss me goodbye then."

I followed her to the door. She took the fiver off me and put it back in her purse. "Sorry, Bo," she said. "It's all we've got. I won't be long. I'll bring you back a sandwich or something."

And then she was gone.

I pretended to be putting the money in my pocket when I walked back in. I didn't want Isabel thinking anything about anything.

Five (Sam)

The old lady on the ground floor was nocturnal and so was her dog, probably through habit rather than choice, because she walked it in the middle of the night. I know because that's how we met, on my eighth day. She got locked out at half past four in the morning. I believed her at the time anyway. She was the first person to speak to me in my new life.

There was a park just round the corner. I learned to call it a park, but actually it was a patch of grass with two benches and some bushes and a bin for dog shit. It was also an open-air crack house. Isabel told me, but she clearly didn't care. She'd been there the night I had to let her in. She threw stones at my window. I thought I'd dreamed them.

"Oi!" she said in this shouting sort of whisper. "Country! Get down here and open the door."

I had to put some clothes on. The stairs were cold and gritty under my feet and I could hardly see. I thought I might still be asleep. She stood there on the doorstep like I'd shown up three hours late to collect her.

"Doesn't anyone brush their hair any more?" she said.

It felt strange, someone talking to me, like having a spotlight shined in my eyes.

"How long've you been here?" she said.

I had to clear my throat to speak, like it was rusty. "I just got up," I said.

"No, Einstein, how long've you *lived* here?" she said.

"Oh. About ten days."

"I haven't seen you," she said, like that meant I was lying. She was feeling about for her spare key above the doorframe but she wasn't quite tall enough to reach.

"Well, I've been here," I said. "I've been keeping to myself." I got the key for her.

She looked me up and down and laughed once. "Pink lung disease."

"What?"

"Pink lung disease. Don't you young people know anything?"

She told me about this policeman at the dawn of the motor age who got sent from his village to do traffic duty in Piccadilly. He wasn't any good at directing traffic. Nobody was because it was a new thing. The policeman got hit by a car and he died. The doctor who cut him up had never seen healthy, pink, country lungs before. He was used to city lungs, all black and gooey, so he said that was the cause of it. Pink lung disease. Not a car driving over him at all.

She looked at me the whole time she was talking. She was the very first person to see me since I'd been here. I was conscious of it.

"You've got lovely country skin," she said. "Look at the glow on you."

"Thanks," I said, because I didn't know how else to take it.

"You stick out like a sore thumb with that healthy skin."

"No I don't," I said.

"Put that key back for me, would you?" she said, and I reached up and put it back above the doorframe. She noticed my watch. It has a thick strap. I always wear it. "What's the time?" she said.

"Four thirty-six."

"Well, what are you standing here for, at that hour?" she said, and she sent me back to my room and shut the door behind her, like she'd forgotten I was only standing there because of her.

I couldn't go back to sleep. Someone was boiling a kettle in the flat upstairs. I heard the plug going into the socket, the switch click to ON, the thrum of the water bubbling on the counter top. I heard an alarm clock somewhere beep seventeen and a half times and then stop. I heard the scrape and warble of pigeons waking up on the windowsill.

I pictured the walls and ceilings and floors separating everyone in their little boxes. I thought about how thin they were, and what might be between them, like dust and mice and lost letters, like feathers and crumbling plaster and hundred-year-old wallpaper. I thought about everyone in the whole city, alone in our boxes like squares on graph paper, like scales on a fish, like ants.

Now I was an ant, maybe Max would've liked to study me, navigating my way round the Tube, walking down a crowded street without colliding, stacking shelves and watching them empty again, sweeping my floor, putting the rubbish out.

Do ants know that they are working for the colony? That whatever little job they get to do until they die actually forms a meaningful part of the whole? *Do* they know that? Because I certainly didn't.

Have you ever done that thing where you interrupt a line of ants? They're all moving along, no questions asked, filled with a sense of purpose, and you draw a line across their path in the mud or the sand or whatever, just a line, with a stick or your shoe or an empty vinegar bottle. The ants in front of the line carry on like nothing happened, like there's nothing to worry about. They don't look back. But the ones behind the line, the ones who walk into it, they lose the plot. It's like they all go insane and run around tearing their hair out because they've got no idea what the hell they're supposed to be doing. Like they've forgotten everything they ever knew.

Max hated it when I did that. It drove him crazy.

That's what I was wondering, sitting in my room listening to other people who didn't know that I existed. If Max was watching me then from above, what side of the line in the ants was I on?

A few nights later I bumped into the old lady again in the hallway. It wasn't late. I was going out for some air because I'd been in my room all day. She came out of her flat just before I got to the front door.

"Ah, Country," she said. "Come in, meet the neighbours."

I didn't want to meet anyone. I shook my head. "No thanks," I said, and I opened the door. I could see a slice of blackish, street-lit sky. I could smell the warm metal and dust of outside.

"You've got to meet the neighbours," she said.

"No, it's all right."

The door was properly open now. Two people walked past on the street, a man and a woman, and they glanced up at me in the light of the hall for less than a second. My shadow was long down the front steps.

She said, "What are you on about, 'No, it's all right'? It's the rules. I have to introduce you."

I said I'd rather she didn't.

"What do you mean?"

She was standing in the doorway now and I was halfway to the pavement. I couldn't really see her face because the light was behind her.

"I don't want to meet the neighbours," I said.

"Suit yourself," she said. She pushed the door shut in front of her, its rectangle of light on the street disappearing in one quick, diminishing movement.

"I will," I said to nobody at all.

I wasn't out for long. I walked about. I sat on a bench at the canal. I watched people in cafes and bars to see what they were doing with their time. I got a newspaper and stared at some TV through the window at Dixons for a bit.

When I got back the lights were still on at the old lady's house. I could see them from the street. Inside, the door to her flat was open. I heard her moving around, heard the muffled sound of her voice and the tap of the dog's feet somewhere, like fingers on a table. I leaned my head against the edge of the front door and watched the sky slice squeeze to nothing while I closed it without making a sound.

"What's your name, anyway?" she said suddenly close behind me, before I'd even turned around.

"God, you made me jump," I said.

"Sorry," she said. She asked me my name again.

"Sam."

She repeated it, like she was testing it for something.

"I'm Isabel," she said. "Meet the neighbours for five minutes and I won't ask you to do anything ever again."

What a good liar.

Her place was crowded and tiny, like someone had pushed the walls together after she'd moved her furniture in, like the storeroom of a bad antique shop.

Steve was there, the landlord, wearing sunglasses inside, something I think you're allowed to hold against a person as soon as you meet them. The dog was in one chair, his nose tucked down between the arm and the cushion, the whites of his eyes new moons as he glanced up at me and breathed out hard with pure boredom. In the other chair there was a hungry-looking bloke with a big pale beard his face was way too small for. He frowned at me and licked his lips, which looked lost in the middle of all that hair. His sweatshirt was the colour of dead grass. He had a full size tattoo of a gun on the side of his calf. It was poking out of his sock like it was a holster. I couldn't keep my eyes off it once I knew it was there.

And on the arm of his chair there was a woman called Cherry, thin and blonde and pretty, and just about the tiredest person I ever saw. Her nails were bitten so low, so close to where they started, I couldn't look at them. Her fingers were covered in rings.

Isabel introduced me as Country. Steve nodded at me behind his shades and clinked the ice cubes in his glass. Cherry waved with one hand and covered a yawn with the other.

"Mick," the man in the chair said. "You walked in on me in the bathroom the other day."

Steve said to Mick, "You probably woke him up the night before chucking your stuff out of the window."

"Sorry," I said, and he grunted at Steve, something about getting a lock on the door that worked.

"Oh, cheer up, Mick," Isabel said. "There's always someone worse off than you. Take Country here. Not a friend in the world."

"Really?" Mick said, perking up a bit, like this was good news.

"Not a soul," Isabel said, patting me on the arm.

She started explaining where everybody lived: Steve in the basement, her on the ground floor, me and the bathroom on the next, Mick on the third floor and Cherry and her daughter at the top.

"Welcome to the madhouse," Steve said, and drained his glass.

There was a silence then that I wasn't going to fill. Cherry stared out of the window, chewing at her nails. Isabel said she was going to get me a drink. Steve followed her out.

Cherry lit a cigarette and dragged on it like there was something at the very end she was looking for. She had too much make-up on. When she brought her hand up to her mouth it looked like somebody else's hand entirely, somebody paler and older.

Mick said to nobody in particular, "Why are we here?"

I didn't know if he meant there, in Isabel's room, or in London, or even alive, and I had no idea of how to answer him.

I got up and tried to see out of the windows. There was a spiral staircase down to a tiny yard, like five hay bales side by side. There were window boxes crammed with rain-bashed petunias. Inside, Isabel's sofas matched the curtains and the carpet was a pond-weed green. There were a couple of paintings on the walls, of ships and insipid landscapes, and they might have some value to an old lady, but they didn't mean anything to me. The most interesting thing in the room by a mile was a clay head on top of a bookcase, a peaceful man with a wide nose and closed eyes. I liked the tight curl of his hair, the fingerprint marks of the hands that had made him on his skin.

Isabel came back with the drinks and sat down in the chair next to Doormat. I stayed standing until she told me to stop it and then I knelt on the floor.

There were crisps in a bowl on the coffee table. I didn't eat that many because the sound of them was too loud in my head and I didn't want to fill the room with crunching. Mick was on to them like only he knew it was the last meal in the building. Little bits of crisp littered his beard like dandruff.

Isabel said there were more in the kitchen and he should go and get them.

Mick looked like his bones were melting. "Can't the new boy do it?"

"No, he can't," Isabel said. "And his name is Country."

I wanted to leave. "My name is Sam," I said, but nobody took any notice.

"Have you eaten?" Isabel said to Cherry.

It took her a long time to react, like she was in slow motion, or moving underwater. She dragged her stare away from middle distance, like there was something fascinating happening there, even though the rest of us couldn't see it.

"Not hungry," she said, scratching at the inside of her elbow.

Isabel frowned and looked over at Steve.

"Communal spaces," he said, like that would mean something.

Mick looked at him and said, "What?"

"I've got the paint and a friend with a bit of spare carpet, but we'll have to do it together."

"Do what together?"

"Decorate the hallway," Isabel said. "Don't you think, Country? It's shocking out there."

I didn't say anything. I was trying to work out how long it would be before I could get up and go. I was wondering how long a person can be in a room and guarantee to make no impression. I didn't want to stay too long and get remembered.

"What about you, Cherry? You going to help?" Steve said.

"Help what?" Cherry said. "I wasn't listening."

Mick stood up then and said, "Are we done?" His gun tattoo flexed when he straightened his legs.

"If you like," Isabel said.

"Well then," he said. "I've got to go and see a man about a dog."

Cherry said, "Can I come?"

But he shook his head and said, "Not that kind of dog, darling. Sorry."

She watched the space in the room he'd left behind, and while she did, Isabel and Steve started questioning me. I should have got up and left with him.

Isabel started. "So tell me what you're doing here, come on."

What was I supposed to say? Running away. Starting from scratch. Hiding.

I shrugged. "I don't know really."

"Where're you from?"

"You wouldn't know it. It's tiny."

"How old are you?"

"Seventeen."

Isabel asked if I was a student.

Cherry said, "Is this *Twenty Questions*?"

I said, "I'm not a student. No."

"Didn't think so. You don't look like one," Isabel said. "They wear silly tight trousers with the arse down by the knees and shoes your feet would freeze in, and hair in their eyes on purpose. You look more ordinary than that."

"I'm very ordinary," I said, and I wanted it to be true and a lie at the same time.

"Animal, vegetable or mineral?" Cherry said, and she laughed at her own joke and went back to looking at nothing.

Doormat suddenly sat up and looked towards the door, down the hallway. We all looked where he was looking, except for Cherry, and there was a knock on the door. I've heard that about dogs; that they know five minutes before you get there that you're on your way home, that they can sense you.

Steve got up to answer it and then I heard footsteps on the carpet, light, barefoot and quick, and there was this kid in the room, scratching at her head, in a pair of really grubby pyjamas that were about three sizes too small.

It was weird her suddenly arriving like that. She looked out of place. I knew her straightaway.

She was the kid I saw before, the day I arrived. She was the girl from the doorway. She was less of an oil painting than I remembered, grey pale with shadows under her eyes, but still that red hair. Doormat was wagging his stumpy little tail at her.

"Hello," Isabel said. "What woke you up?"

"Dunno," she said, and she was frowning hard at me because I was new.

"This is Sam," Isabel said. "Sam, this is Bo, Cherry's little girl."

At the mention of her name, Cherry looked over at her and smiled. "What you doing down here?" she said.

"Can't sleep."

Cherry carried on smiling, but she didn't move. The girl came up and stood next to her, leaning her back against the tip of Cherry's folded knee. She looked at me without blinking.

I looked back.

"I've seen you before," I said.

"She lives here," Steve said.

"No, before," I said. "I saw you before. The day I arrived."

"I've seen that Andrew Marr before," Isabel said, "on the Tube, but that doesn't change anything."

"Where'd you see me?" the girl said. Her voice was wiry and reed thin.

"On the High Street," I said. "You looked like a painting."

She snorted. "A *what*?"

"Ignore him, Bo," Cherry said without looking at either of us. She was lighting another cigarette and her voice was hard through her clamped jaw. "He's trying to chat you up."

The pale of the girl's face blushed in an instant.

"No, I'm not," I said. "What is she, eight?"

Cherry smiled in my direction, an exhausted, joyless smile.

"I'm *ten*," the girl said, like it was obvious to everyone but me.

She didn't look ten. I knew kids who were six that were bigger than her.

"Was it a nice painting?" the girl asked.

"Yes," I said.

"Well, that's OK then."

She was still leaning into Cherry. Isabel asked her if she was hungry. The girl shook her head. "I'm cold."

"Do you want a hot drink?"

"OK."

Steve was in the kitchen, banging ice cubes into another drink. Isabel called out, "Steve, warm some up milk for her, would you?"

Cherry had one arm loosely around her daughter and her head bent low, like she'd fallen asleep.

"What's she eaten today?" Isabel said. "Apart from what I've given her."

"Lobster thermidor," Cherry said, and the girl giggled.

I felt uncomfortable in there, like I was watching things I shouldn't. "I'm going," I said.

"Don't be silly," Isabel said. "Have another drink."

Cherry held her glass out for whoever felt like taking it. She lit another cigarette and closed her eyes. "I'm going too," she said, but she didn't move.

Steve was a bit unsteady on his feet. He sat down heavily when he came back in, slopped hot milk on to Doormat. He kept reaching out to ruffle the kid's hair. You could see she didn't like it.

I looked at Cherry, and she had her eyes open and she was watching me. "What's your name again?" she said.

"Sam."

She asked me if I had any fags. I said I didn't smoke.

"Got any blow?" she said.

"No, sorry."

She stopped talking to me then. We sat in the room like we were all alone. The girl finished her drink and put her arms back round Cherry, kind of between her waist and the arm of the chair. It looked awkward. Cherry put one hand out and stroked the girl's hair. Her eyes moved behind closed lids, flickered beneath the surface like someone dreaming.

I reminded myself I hadn't wanted to meet these people. I told myself I was free to leave. So I did.

"So nice of you to pop round," Isabel said at the door, like any of it had been my idea.

I wrote a letter in my head.

Dear Mum,

How are you? I am living with a bunch of freaks.

The Story of My Life
Part One
by B Hoban

Mum says we come from a long line of Romany Gypsies and that's why we can't stay in one place because it's in our blood to keep moving. She says that was the trouble with my dad, that he was cemented to the floor. She says her granny was the first ever Hoban woman to live in a house. And our real name isn't even Hoban, it's a secret, but Bohemia was my great great grandad who was a handsome and magnificent horse thief.

I asked her if she gave me a boy's name cos she wished I'd been a boy. She said it would've been easier in a lot of ways, but a name's a name. "Look at me," she said. "I've been stuck with Cherry all my life."

What I remember first is the big place, The Haven. It was a huge red house and it had peacocks in the garden. There was a white pony in the field behind. It didn't like me. It was allergic to grass. If it ate grass, its tummy swelled up like a balloon, so it wasn't allowed any. I think that's why it didn't like me, cos it couldn't eat its favourite thing and it had to take that out on somebody.

The Haven was Uncle Derek's. He was old and he wasn't my uncle. I didn't see much of Mum then, or I don't remember. I don't know how long we were there for, but it felt like a long time. There weren't any other children ever. Derek's children were all grown up and anyway they didn't come round.

There was a nice lady called Mrs Betty who put me to bed and woke me up and played with me and made me ride the fat pony who didn't like me. Mrs Betty had a really red face, like she'd always just climbed a hill, and she wore those sock tights that only go up to your knee. I didn't like it when the tops of her sock tights showed, and her real leg was all blue and marbly.

Uncle Derek was rich. Mum told me he made his money out of tights. That made me think of Mrs Betty and her socks, and if Derek was responsible for them. It's funny the things you can get rich on, like tights and Post-it notes and tea-towel holders that look like animals' bottoms.

Mum went to be a model for his tights and that's how they met. According to her, he took one look at her legs and fell in love with her. Mum's sister Suzie said that's the sort of thing Mum lives for, some part of her anatomy changing a man's life. Mum said she was just jealous cos she lived in a fat boring house with a fat boring man and three fat boring kids. I wasn't supposed to hear any of that. We didn't see Suzie for a while after. Mum said just because you have a fat boring sister doesn't mean you have to like her.

Six (Sam)

After that night at Isabel's house, after meeting the neighbours, I kept out of everyone's way. It wasn't hard. I didn't leave my room if I heard voices or people in the corridor. If I heard the front door go I checked who it was coming in or going out. I timed my movements. I got good at reading the sounds through the walls and ceilings and floors.

It was Monday, maybe about a week since I'd seen any of them. I was going to the shop to check my shifts, maybe pick up some cans of soup and out of date milk, stuff like that. It wasn't far. I cut through the little park opposite the end of the street, walked round the back of the high street, turned left and walked in.

This boy Besnik was at the counter. It was his uncle's place. He was nice enough to me, though I'm not sure he remembered my name between one meeting and the next. He mainly talked about girls and the plans he had for his car, to whoever his uncle was paying to listen.

But Besnik wasn't talking about cars today. He was pointing at one of the mirrors in the corner of the shop, one that meant you could see the whole place like you were looking at it through a fish bowl.

"Sssht!" he said, putting his index finger up to my face, not taking his eyes off the mirror. "I've got one."

"One what?" I said, looking up the mirror, not making out all that much.

"A thief. Look! Look!"

He banged his finger against the screen of the little CCTV monitor by the till. I could see less on that than I could on the mirror. It was fuzzy and jumpy and grey.

Besnik loved shoplifters. You'd have thought his uncle set the whole business up just to attract them, that catching them was what a shop was all about.

"Two Vodka Mules and a packet of Pringles," he said. "So far."

"Breakfast of Champions," I said, but he ignored me.

"I'm going to bury her," he said, his attention whipping between the mirror and the screen like it was life or death, like he was bringing a plane in to land.

The thing Besnik liked best about thieves was being in the right. He'd have made a really good policeman or headmaster or something. I told him that.

"Too short," he said. "Too short, too boring, too dangerous."

I wondered what wasn't boring or dangerous about working in an all night grocer's in Camden Town, but I didn't argue. At least he was right about the short thing. Besnik came up to about my armpit and he was a couple of years older than me. So he got his kicks scaring the shit out of people who stole cheese and baked beans and cider, threatening them with a baseball bat, chasing them into the market, calling the police. I didn't want to be around to see it.

"Any old milk?" I said.

"Out the back. Don't take it all."

"No," I said. "That would be stealing."

He scowled at me and then he went back to staring at the shoplifter.

I had to go round the counter to get into the back. I had to cross the width of the shop to the corner, and then duck under it and go through a beaded curtain into the stockroom, which smelled of yoghurt and mice. I looked right when I got to the corner, so I could see who Besnik was watching so intently on his monitor, who was next in his one-man battle against petty crime.

It was the girl.

She had her back to the rest of the shop and her hands in her pockets and her head down. I still knew who it was, the silly little kid.

I looked from her to Besnik and back to her again. Neither of them was looking at me. I kept close to the shelves and walked towards her, staying out of the corner so I wouldn't show up on the CCTV.

What I needed was for someone else to come in, for the bell on the door to go, that infuriating electric one that buried itself in your skull and played out again later, hours after your shift, when it was least welcome, when you thought you had at least twelve hours before you had to hear it again.

Bing Bang Bong.

A woman came in with a pushchair and a noisy toddler. I looked behind me. Besnik was trying to watch the monitor, but the toddler's little hands were all over the sweets, and the mum wanted three lottery cards and some fags and a load of other stuff she kept remembering and banging on the counter.

"Psst!" I said, and the girl ignored me.

"Bo! Put it back," I said. "He's watching you."

She turned and looked at me, and something like terror crossed her face, mixed with a smile.

"I'm not joking. I know him. I work here."

When I said that she nodded quickly without looking round, and she took a bottle out of each sleeve and put them back on the shelf.

I quickly ducked under the counter before Besnik saw me. When I came back out with the milk, the woman had gone and Bo was paying for the Pringles in 2ps with her sleeves rolled up, all innocence. Besnik was fuming. You could tell he felt cheated.

"See you," I said to him, and I left before her.

I didn't wait for her. Saving her skin was enough of a favour. I didn't want to have to talk to her as well. But she came skittering up behind me with this nervous laugh.

"Thanks," she said, and she smiled like we were in on it together.

"You're mad," I said.

She offered me a Pringle.

"I don't know how you can eat those," I said.

"I like them. Do you really work in there?"

I said I did, and that if I lost my job because of her stealing I'd be seriously annoyed.

"I didn't steal anything," she said.

"Only because I stopped you."

It was quiet for about five paces and then she said, "You must nick *loads* of stuff from there if you work there."

"No," I said.

She shrugged. "My mum gets everything from places where she works. Loo roll, cocktail sticks, hand soap..."

I interrupted her. "Where's she work now?"

"I don't know," she said. "The pub on our street maybe. Sometimes. I'm not sure."

"I'll warn them."

She looked up at me and stopped walking. "Don't do that," she said.

"OK," I said. "But don't take stuff in there. You'll get caught."

"All right."

"And what are you nicking vodka for?"

"For my mum. For when she gets back."

"Well, that's sweet of you. Where is she?"

Bo shrugged. Her mouth was crammed full of chive and onion or whatever it was. She couldn't get them in fast enough. "Did you have breakfast?" she asked, waving the tube at me. "I'm having it now."

"That's not breakfast."

She had to walk really fast to keep up with me. Her trainers scudded on the floor and left her feet just a little bit with every step. She finished the crisps and put the tube half sticking out of her pocket and she ate the flavour off all of her fingers.

She said, "I'm going to make a pencil case with this when I get in. These make great pencil cases."

The front door was open and the carpet was wet, from rain or maybe something else, I didn't want to know. It squelched a bit under our feet and Bohemia made a pattern in it like a flower, her wet footprint petals fading away as fast as she could make them.

I said I was going upstairs.

"OK," she said, and she carried on treading. She watched the disappearing flowers while she talked. "My mum'll be back soon," she said. "Any minute."

I went back to my room and I did a bit of sweeping. I didn't think about the girl again that day, or the one after that. That's the kind of person I must be – I never think about things I care about until I've lost them.

Seven (Bohemia)

Mum was under the covers in all her clothes and her shoes were sticking out at the end of the sofa, still on her feet. They were my favourites, dark blue with little holes, and they looked really pretty lying there.

I took about £2 out of her purse and I went to the shop for some milk and something to eat. Mum gets cross if there's no milk in the morning for her tea. When I came back, Isabel was sweeping. She was wearing an apron and flip-flops and her feet looked really blue and old.

She asked me what I was doing with my day, seeing as I wasn't in school, and cos I hadn't decided yet I didn't answer. I asked about the new boy. I said I remembered him from before, at Isabel's. I didn't tell her about the stealing. I'm not a total idiot.

She said, "Sam? Maybe he could give you lessons. He dresses badly enough to be clever."

I hadn't been thinking about lessons, but I had thought it would be good to know someone closer to my age, someone who wasn't Steve or Isabel, cos if you added them up you got about a hundred and thirty-nine.

Obviously I didn't say that. I said, "Tell me about him then."

Isabel said that for once she didn't know that much, and then she winked at me and tapped the side of her nose. "I'm working on it. Maybe you can help me."

When we knocked on his door, I don't think he was all that pleased to see us. It took him ages to answer. I said maybe he was out and we should go away, but Isabel said she wasn't going anywhere because she knew he was in there.

"I'm asleep!" he shouted after about a hundred knocks.

"Well, wake up then," Isabel said. "For God's sake, do something with your life."

He opened the door. I don't know what he thought when he saw us standing there.

"Where've you been?" Isabel said.

"What do you mean?" he said. I think he was annoyed.

She said, "Someone's been looking for you."

He seemed to wake up then. "Who?" he said, and he looked past us and down the stairs.

Isabel smiled. “Don’t panic,” she said. “It’s just Bohemia here,” and I smiled at him with my smile full of holes.

“Bohemia?”

I hate when people do that, say my name again because they can’t have heard right.

I nodded and smiled harder because I didn’t know what else to do.

“She wants to play,” Isabel said.

“You’re joking, right?” Sam said, but he wasn’t laughing.

“Come on,” Isabel said. “She’s bored to death.”

This was a lie cos I just can’t get bored. Some people can’t lie or roll their tongues into a sausage or lift one eyebrow or say one sentence without using the f-word. I can’t get bored. There’s always too much to think about.

Sam said, “Are you serious?”

“Yes. Go and play. Take Doormat with you. He’s desperate too.”

He banged his head three times against the doorframe, just hard enough.

“He doesn’t want to,” I said, and I tried to turn away, but Isabel had my hand and she wouldn’t let go.

“You realise you woke me up,” Sam said.

Isabel said she meant to. “Sleep when you’re old.”

“What if I say no?” he said.

I said, "It's OK. You don't have to."

"You'll hurt her feelings," Isabel said. "I wouldn't do that."

Sam said, "Well, why don't you take her then?"

"Because I'm *old*," she said. "Bohemia doesn't want to spend the day with someone old, do you, dear?"

"Not really," I said. "No offence."

He looked at Doormat. "*He's* old as well. How far can *he* go?"

Isabel said, "He's a dog, Country, not a wind-up toy." I laughed at that.

"OK," he said, looking at me. "I'll take them to the Heath, but that's it."

I tried smiling again, but he just looked at me and sighed like this wasn't the day he'd been hoping for.

Isabel gave him a bag with some things for Doormat – a little jacket for if he got cold and a thing that must have once been a tennis ball, but was more like glue and wet carpet. I wasn't touching that.

"Good," she said, putting my hand into Sam's and giving me the lead to hold. "Neither of you goes out enough in daylight."

When Isabel started off down the stairs, Sam told me to wait right there and he followed. I heard what he said. He asked her if it wasn't a bit weird, a total stranger taking a kid out for a walk.

"You're hardly a stranger. We all know where you live."

He said, "You don't know anything about me. I could be dangerous."

She laughed. "Well, are you?"

"No," he said. "I don't know."

She said, "What's weird about being nice to a child with no friends and not enough vitamin D? I've heard of worse."

He said he wasn't a childminder.

"No," said Isabel. "You're far too *dangerous* for that."

Me and Doormat had to wait outside while he got dressed.

On the way down the stairs, Sam said that Doormat might not be a wind-up toy but he looked like one, and it was true. The way he bumped and scuffled down the front steps made me laugh.

I said I wondered what it was like living in London with your belly that close to the ground.

"Unhygienic," Sam said, and I wasn't sure what it meant exactly, but I knew it wasn't comfortable.

"Does your mum know where we're going?" he said.

I was still watching Doormat bounce down. "She's asleep. She won't be up for ages."

He said, "Do you want to leave her a note? Tell her where you are?"

"I don't need to."

Isabel came back out to the doorstep. She waved a fiver at us. Sam went back up the steps to get it.

"What's this, my wages?" he said. I wished he hadn't.

Isabel said, "It's for you to get them an ice cream."

"*Them*?"

"Doormat likes ninety-nines."

We walked to the end of the street without talking, his big steps and my quicker ones, and Doormat's claws tap-tapping on the concrete the fastest of all. My trainers looked a bit scruffy, but I'd done this careful rolling thing with my socks that kind of made up for it.

"When did you move in?" I said, and I looked up at him. Sam had dark hair and outdoors skin, and he was tall in a way that made my neck ache from looking.

"Not long ago," he said without looking at me.

"Who do you live with? Mum or Dad or both?"

He said he lived on his own.

"Isn't that lonely?" I said.

"No, it's just alone."

Sam liked that word. He said it a lot. I know he didn't want to be with me and Doormat at all. He wanted to be ALONE. Sam was like the opposite of me. I like to be surrounded by people.

Later, in the park, I shivered and shivered until he let

me borrow his sweatshirt. It was huge, like a dress, and it was warm and smelled kind of boyish and oily. His T-shirt underneath said FDNY and on the back it said STAY BACK 200 FEET. I asked him what FDNY stood for.

"Fire Department New York," he said.

I said, "Are you a fireman?" And he laughed and said he just liked the shirt cos 200 FEET was about as close as he wanted people to get.

See what I mean? ALONE.

While we walked he wasn't doing any of the talking so I had to.

"How old are you?" I said.

"Seventeen."

"I'm ten. If you add us together, you'd get my mum."

He said, "Cherry."

"Yes," I said. "You met her the other night."

"She seemed all right."

"Thanks," I said, cos I think he meant it in a good way. "She is." And then I shouldn't have done, but I said, "But not in the mornings. My mum doesn't like mornings."

"Fair enough."

"Or Mondays, or policemen, or marzipan, or bills, or me doing too much talking..."

"You? Doing too much talking?" he said.

I nodded. "And I'm supposed to call her Cherry cos she doesn't like the M word."

"The what?"

"M-u-m. It makes her feel old. I'm not allowed to use it."

We hadn't got very far on account of the length of Doormat's legs. Sam said he could picture him giving out on the lead from too much exercise. Actually it was quite worrying cos the poor dog looked done in already with his tongue hanging out sideways and his tiny teeth showing in a smile.

"Maybe we should get the bus," he said.

"We'd probably have to wait ages."

Plus we only had the money for ice cream and I really wanted one of those.

Sam said he just thought the dog might like a lift so I picked him up and put him like a doll in the bend of my arm. "There," I said, and Doormat put his wet nose against my skin and started sniffing. It was cold and wet and it tickled, like a living, breathing mushroom.

"He likes you," Sam said.

I lifted Doormat higher and rubbed my cheek in his fur. "We're best friends," I said. "Aren't we, boy? Yes, we are."

The park was freezing and the ice creams made it worse. Doormat walked with his nose practically glued to the ground, just *sniffing*. Sam wanted to go into the woods. He said even though he got sick of the sight of trees at home, he quite wanted to be in some now.

I said, "Where did you live?" And he told me but I'd never heard of it.

Suddenly on the path there were hundreds of ants. Thousands. They'd kicked up this dust all around the edge of the stones, like they were trying to move them or something.

"Ooh," I said. "How weird is that?"

Sam got right down to have a proper look. "*Myrmica rubra*," he said.

"What's that mean?" I said.

"Red ant."

I asked him how he knew. I love it when people know stuff out of the blue like that and then I get to know it too.

"Myrmecology," he said, and he grinned at me like I should know what he was on about.

"Murmur-what?" I said.

"Myrmecology. It means the study of ants."

It was like looking down at people from a helicopter. "It's like rush hour," I said,

"That's exactly what it's like," Sam said.

We were crouched down staring at them. They were all so *busy* and knowing where they were going. I said Isabel would boil a kettle and pour it all over them if she saw ants running around like that. I said I'd seen her doing it on the front steps before, to those ants that get wings and all fly about like an ant-cloud on only one day of the year.

"She shouldn't do that," he said.

"Why not?"

"She just shouldn't. Ants are pretty incredible creatures. If you knew Max you'd never boil an ant to death again."

"Who's Max?"

Sam said it was just someone he grew up with. He said he was like an ant expert and he knew about all different types and what they could do. He said Max knew pretty much everything about everything.

"Cool. What a good friend to have," I said.

He said, "Did you know, that the weight of all the ants in the world is the same as the weight of all the humans?"

I asked him how anyone could know that.

"It's a fact," he said.

"Who's weighed them all?" I said. "How can you weigh something like that?"

He looked at me funny. Then he said it was also a fact that even though there were thousands and thousands of different kinds of ant out there, they still hadn't finished finding new ones.

I said that didn't make sense. Cos if they haven't found

them yet, how would they know they're there? I said, "And how did they weigh them all if they haven't found them yet?"

He laughed at me then, and even though I hadn't meant it to be funny I was glad that it was.

He let an ant crawl up on to his hand. "You should meet Max," he said. "He'd like you."

"OK. When?"

"I don't know," he said, putting the ant back and watching it scurry around at mad angles. "I don't know when I'll be seeing him again."

"How come?"

All he said was, "Long story," like I didn't have time to listen, like I was busy doing other things.

After the woods, which were warmer out of the wind and patchy with light, he kept worrying about my mum, about her worrying. I wished he wouldn't.

He said, "She's going to wake up and you're not there."

"She won't wake up," I said.

"She will at some point."

"Well, she won't worry."

He looked at me funny then, like he didn't believe me. "All mums worry."

I shrugged and rubbed Doormat's back. He'd worn himself

out with sniffing. We were going to have to carry him all the way home. "Mine doesn't, honest."

When I asked Sam about his mum and dad he said they weren't really speaking at the moment. We were sitting on the grass outside the playground. I quite wanted to go in, but I didn't want to leave him on his own outside so I didn't.

"How come?" I said.

He sort of laughed to himself and said, "Right now they don't like me."

"Are they cross with you?" I said.

"Yes."

"Did you have a big fight?"

"Not really."

"Are you cross with *them*?"

"No," he said. "Maybe."

He lay back on the grass and closed his eyes. I lay down next to him and I kept my hand on Doormat just in case by some miracle he got the energy to try and run away.

The Story of My Life
Part Two
by B Hoban

After The Haven we lived in William's house that William hardly ever lived in. It was a big flat in a big block of flats near to *Harrods.*

William was a friend of Derek's, but I don't think he had anything to do with tights. Actually, Mum said William didn't have anything to do full-stop cos all his money was just there waiting for him when he was born, which must be weird. Mum said William's money stopped him from being good at much at all, apart from spending it. His flat was a really hard place to be clumsy in cos everything was white or nearly white and if you tripped carrying a cup of chocolate milk, your life was *over.* Mum liked it there though cos all she had to do was make it nice for when William came to visit, which was every Tuesday and sometimes on the weekends if his wife was away. The rest of the time Mum just pretended it was hers and had her friends round and drank William's wine and spent William's money on bras.

On Tuesdays and Sundays I had to be not seen and not heard. When William stayed the night I had to have enough food in my room to last for breakfast, and enough pens and paper and things to do. I wasn't allowed to make a sound. Mum said we couldn't put a foot wrong or we'd be out on the street. Mum said I was a big secret and she was going to surprise William with me sooner or later.

It turned out I was putting both my feet wrong just by being alive cos when Mum surprised him he definitely wasn't pleased about it. She was angry for weeks about that.

We went to stay with her friend Nancy in an attic. All the houses round there were huge and looked like pictures on a chocolate box, white with black wood patterns on the outside. There were lots of them all the same and inside each one was about thirty flats, and it was only girls who lived there, which Mum said was weird and like living on another planet. She didn't say that in front of Nancy though cos I think Nancy liked girls best of all.

I liked it there in the daylight cos there were other kids to play with and the park was close. But sometimes at night Mum and Nancy locked me in and went to work at the Casino.

They were always very pretty when they left. Mum's hair didn't feel like hair and her lipstick was sealed and shiny like a rain mac and the same colour as her nails. Sirens got suddenly louder when she wasn't there, and planes, and small noises outside and in the hallways that you probably wouldn't notice if you weren't by yourself – doors and footsteps and voices. I spent the whole time working out how I would escape if there was a fire or a burglar or something.

Once I could hear somebody breathing right there in the room, I swear I could, and it wasn't me cos I was hardly breathing at all. I couldn't move. I could hardly even blink cos I knew he would hear me.

Every night Mum did the same thing, which was make me drink my milk and close my eyes and tell me not open them again until she got back. Maybe it was my fault cos I always opened them as soon as she was gone.

Eight (Sam)

You couldn't get a dog more different to mine than Doormat. My dog was called Ringo, a massive black thing ten times the size. He could have eaten him for breakfast, but he was terrified of small yappy dogs so Doormat might have had the upper hand.

I told Bohemia about Ringo while she was walking along with Doormat in her arms. I said, "You'd never carry him, but he might give you a ride on his back."

"Nuh-uh," she said. "No thanks."

We played this game of hers while we were walking, called three favourites. We had to, apparently. She picked a category and I had to give my three favourite fruits or colours or TV shows or whatever. I tried to explain that you can only have one favourite thing really, by definition, but she just looked at me blankly and said, "I can have as many favourite anythings as I want. It's a *game*."

Bohemia's favourite dogs were Chihuahua, King Charles and Daschund, and mine were Labrador, Wolfhound and anything, because I didn't care. We had to choose meals and drinks and books and songs, and I thought it would never end. The last one she said was people.

"Who's your three favourite people?" she said. "Mine's my mum and Isabel and you."

I told her not to be ridiculous. I said she'd only met me once. I said, "I could be really horrible – you haven't known me long enough to find out."

She said, "None of my friends are horrible."

I said I didn't have any favourite people. I said I didn't have any friends. I said I moved to London to get away from people, and she laughed and said, "That's just *dumb*."

She said, "What about Max?"

"OK, Max," I said.

"And Ringo?"

"Not a person."

"Well pets count."

"OK."

"And me," she said. "You can choose me. I chose you so it's fair."

"OK," I said. "Max and Ringo and Bohemia are my three favourite people."

"That's better," she said.

She said, "Anyway, why would you move to such a crowded place if you wanted to be alone? I just don't *believe* you."

I said I used to walk Ringo a lot on the common near to Max's. We had to walk there and back on the road, which wasn't so nice, but once you got there it was flat and high, right at the foot of the mountain.

"It was full of rabbits," I told Bohemia. "Ringo could knock himself out chasing those."

"What really?"

"No, but he knocked me over once or twice."

I remember one of the farmer's sons was herding wild ponies on his quad bike, driving them down the mountain before the snow came, helping them out. Everything was hazy, light shining through mist, like my eyes weren't focusing properly, like someone hadn't wiped the windscreen.

Max was up there wearing his weird coat. You could spot him from any distance. It was an old fisherman's jacket, bright yellow, ridiculous. It had pockets on the inside that Max had put there. He kept things in it – string, knives, magnifying glass, compass, specimen pots from the doctor. Max in that yellow coat was like a glow-in-the-dark field trip, a walking laboratory. He was certifiable.

I waved and he turned away for a second to look behind him, like he was making sure I wasn't waving at someone else. There was nobody else there in all that open space.

When he got closer I saw he'd cut his hair again. His cheeks were raw pink with the cold. "Hello," I said. "Been to the barber's?"

He touched it with the flat of a hand. It stuck up like clutches of wild grass. I wondered if it felt sharp. "How's it going, Sam?" he said.

I shrugged "OK. Bored. What are you doing?"

"Nothing much."

I said, "You've got your crazy coat on, Max. You've got to be up to something."

"Yep," he said, but he wasn't telling me what it was.

Ringo was chasing the quad bike, barking his head off. We both watched him, shielding our eyes from the sun.

"Still chasing things that could kill him," Max said.

"Yep. Motorbikes, cars, tractors. He's got a thing about being run over."

"Survival instinct," Max said, and I couldn't tell if he was joking. I never could.

The bracken was knee high and there were winding paths through and in between, and you never quite ended up where you were headed. The dog came crashing back through the leaves like a fish jumping out of water. He ran right into the side of my legs because he's an idiot, and he was over-excited and the plants were too high for him to see where he was going. I hit the floor and just lay there with him standing over my face.

"Ouch," Max said.

"Stupid hound."

"Well, nice to see you," he said, not really looking at me, rubbing the dog's back with both hands.

When I rolled over in the crumbling stink and got to my feet, the quad bike was gone. The ponies were moving slowly across the flat, necks down, eight of them together. I brushed broken leaves off my clothes and Max walked away through the bracken in his yellow coat, sending up plumes of plant dust in the light.

"You must miss Max," Bohemia said. "And Ringo."

I said, "I suppose I do."

"Lucky you've got me," she said. "One out of three's not bad."

I looked at her, smiling at me, her legs sticking out of my

sweatshirt like the sticks I've thrown down the river all my life, big-kneed and bleached to bone by the sun. She seriously thought we were friends.

Nine (Bohemia)

When I came downstairs the morning of the power cut, Steve and Isabel were busying about. Steve was painting the wall in the hallway. I asked if I could help.

Isabel said, "You can chuck the junk mail in the recycling. And when we've taken the carpet up, you can give it a good sweep with me."

I said, "Can Doormat stay out here with us?"

"Course he can."

"Won't he escape?"

"No. He knows which side his bread is buttered."

"What does that mean?"

"It means I've been feeding him twice a day for twelve and a half years and he hasn't had to do an ounce of work for it."

I sat in the doorway with all the letters, and the ones with names I didn't know I threw in the bin. I heard Sam coming down the stairs.

"What does that one say?" Isabel asked, pointing at one. Her finger was like a drawing of a stick. "Who's the letter for?"

"The Occupier."

"What about that one?" Isabel said, picking up another. She took it out of my hands. "Oh, that's for you," she said, and she held the envelope out to Sam.

"Can't be," he said.

"Why not?"

Sam shrugged. "It just can't."

"Sam Cassidy," Isabel read. "That's you, isn't it?"

Sam didn't look very happy.

"Come on," Isabel said. "Take it and open it."

He shook his head.

I stood up and took the letter out of Isabel's hand.

"It doesn't say your name," I said. "She's teasing you. It says Sarah Chakrabati." I looked at Isabel cos I knew what she was up to. "I can read, you know."

"Oh," said Isabel, and you could tell she was lying. "I must have the wrong glasses on."

"You're a good little reader," Steve said.

"Thanks."

I heard what Isabel said to Sam while Steve was talking. She said it quietly, but I heard it anyway. She said, "Nobody knows you're here, do they."

Steve cleared his throat and picked his brush back out of the water.

And I thought, *That's rubbish, because I do.*

Later, Mum brought me back a sandwich – a chicken and sweetcorn one – and even though I'd been thinking about being a vegetarian, I was glad cos it was after six by then and I would've eaten a horse with pickle.

She sat down with me on the sofa bed. We hadn't put it away since we moved in and I was trying not to get chicken and sweetcorn on the sheets. When I finished I stood up and brushed the crumbs off me on to the floor.

"You still hungry?" Mum said.

"A bit."

She asked me if I was happy and I said, "Course."

She lifted her arm and I sat back closer to her, right in against her side. It was nice. She had her hand on my hair and it pulled a little bit on my hair band, tweaked something sharp at my neck, but I didn't say anything cos I didn't want her to move.

"I'm sorry I haven't seen you all day," she said, and she kissed the top of my head.

"We cleaned the hallway," I said. "Did you notice?"

She said the lights were off when she came in. She said, "Maybe I smelled paint."

I told her I helped. "Good for you," she said.

She was quiet for a bit and then she got up and went to the loo. She was in there for ages. I kept talking to her to make sure she hadn't fallen asleep.

"Sam lives by himself," I said through the door.

"Who?"

"Sam. He works in a shop down the road. Maybe he could get you a job there."

There was a long wait before Mum said, "Maybe."

I didn't tell her that nobody knew Sam was here. I didn't think she'd want to know.

When she came out she was wearing just her underwear and she was running a bath. Her bare feet made this sliding noise on the floor, like she was walking without picking them up. I got in the bath with her and she didn't mind at all, and we lay there in the bubbles doing nothing. Afterwards she helped me build this sort of roof for the sofa bed out of a blanket hanging and a long piece of string. We tied one end of the string to the wall and one end to a nail in the door, and draped the blanket over it. When the door was shut it was perfect, but if you opened it everything collapsed. You could

sit on the sofa bed like you were in a tent looking out.

She got in the tent with me and we lay there looking out at the walls.

I said, "Maybe we'll go camping for real, in the summer, and build a big fire on the beach and eat fresh fish and marshmallows."

Mum used to love camping when she was a kid. She said, "You had to buy tokens for the shower and when the token ran out that was it. You'd have to go into the shop in your towel with soap everywhere and buy another one."

She said, "We didn't eat fresh fish, we ate beans and sausages out of a can and everything had wet grass in it."

"Let's go," I said. "Do you promise?"

She didn't promise, but she did say she'd stay like that till I was asleep as long as I didn't stay awake on purpose to stop her from moving.

I swear she fell asleep before me.

When I woke up in the night, all the lights were out and she wasn't there. I felt around in the bed for her, but it was empty. It's weird how everything going dark could wake a person who's in the dark anyway with their eyes shut, but it did and that's what happened.

It was like an actual thing, the dark, like a solid. I didn't like it. I thought maybe my tent thing was blocking out the light so I reached out and pulled it to one side, but it was still all black in the room.

"Mum?" I said, a bit quietly, but there wasn't an answer.

"Mum!" I said again, louder this time. "Where are you? It's not funny."

I think I called out one more time, I shouted, and then I heard someone on the stairs and everything about me prickled. They were creeping. I could hear my own blood in my ears. If there'd been a spider in the kitchen cupboard I'd've heard it. If a cat had licked its fur three streets away it would've been deafening. I think my ears were trying to make up for the fact that I was blind. I could hear things moving, above me and below me, and I heard the footsteps again on the stairs, and then someone banged on my door, really loud, and I jumped, even though I'd heard them coming.

"Who's that?" I said.

"It's Sam. Are you all right?"

"I think so," I said.

"You were shouting," he said.

"I was looking for my mum."

"Are you on your own?"

"I don't know," I said.

"What do you mean, you don't know?"

I told him that Mum was here when I went to sleep, but that I couldn't see her now. I felt like crying, sitting there in the blackness trying to explain things through a door I couldn't see.

"Cherry?" he called, but there was no answer.

He said that Isabel sent him to get me. He said, "She banged on my ceiling. She wants you to come down."

I was scared to move. I was scared of what I might bump into or tread on. I felt my way to the door really slowly. When I opened it I still couldn't see anything.

"Why have all the lights gone out?" I said.

"Power cut. Isabel's looking for some candles. I had a torch somewhere, but I can't find it."

I let the door shut behind me without thinking and we went down together.

I hate going on the stairs by myself, even if it's just a little bit dark. If Sam hadn't been with me, every corner would've had someone lurking in it. The blackness behind me would've snuck up and swallowed me whole.

When we hit the bottom I could feel the carpet under my feet. Isabel's door must've been open already cos Sam said, "Here we are," and I don't know how he could see it when I couldn't. Then we were in her hallway and she was coming towards us with a little candle in her hand.

The flame pushed light through the gaps in her fingers, made her face look like a cave. She was wearing a nightie. She looked really, really old.

She said, "Don't you just love a power cut? It reminds me of the war."

"Why?" I said.

"Because of the blackout, dear. We had to stop all the light showing so the enemy planes couldn't find us."

"Is that true?" I said.

"Course it is," she said. "Now, let me have a look at you. Are you all right? Do you want a biscuit or something?"

I said I was fine. I said I was asleep and the lights going off woke me up.

"You're a light sleeper then," she said, "like me."

We stood there in her hallway for a minute, like we were waiting for a bus or something, and then she said, "Where's your mum?"

"I don't know," I said. "She was there before."

"She must be out," Isabel said. "I don't suppose we know when she'll be back?"

How could I when I didn't even know she was going? "No," I said. "I don't suppose we do."

We followed her and her candle into the kitchen. My feet were cold and I tried to tuck them in my pyjama trousers, but if I pulled them so they reached my feet, they only half covered my bum.

"Do you want some socks?" Isabel said.

"All right."

While she was gone to find some there was another knock at the door. Sam got up. "I'll get that," he said.

It was Steve. He was saying something about the whole block being out. Then he said, "I've been upstairs and I can't wake the kid."

He said it just as he walked in the kitchen, and he saw me and we smiled. "Oh, hello," he said. "You're here already."

"Yes, I am."

"If you look outside," he said to Sam, "there's no light anywhere. It's a proper power failure. It's not just us."

We went to the kitchen window and Steve said, "See?" But you couldn't see much of anything, which was the point.

The socks Isabel brought me were big and fluffy and made my feet sweat as soon as I put them on.

"You can keep those," she said. "They make my feet sweat."

I sat cross-legged at the kitchen table while Isabel made hot chocolate. She called her oven a *stove* and she called hot chocolate *cocoa*. When it came it was scalding and not very sweet, and as soon as it wasn't scalding any more it had this horrible thick skin on it that stuck to my lip and looked all crinkly in the candlelight, like Isabel's skin.

Steve poured something out of a little bottle into his.

"Where's Mick?" Isabel asked him, and Steve said he'd been on his way out last time he saw him, but that was ages ago.

"He can't be in," Isabel said. "He'd be down here like a shot. He hates the dark."

It made me laugh, a grown-up being scared of something like that, and Steve looked at me. "What, weren't you scared?"

"Not really," I said. "Maybe a bit."

I couldn't get comfy on the chair and I wanted to go back to sleep so that waiting for the lights to come back on didn't feel like forever. I asked if I could go home.

Isabel said she didn't think so.

"I'll take her," Sam said.

"Are you sure you want to go?" Isabel said to me, and I was.

"I'm tired," I said. "I want to go to sleep."

"You can sleep here," she said.

I said that Mum wouldn't know where I was if I did that.

She said something about a taste of her own medicine. I heard her.

Steve said, "Two wrongs don't make a right."

"Sam'll take you then," she said.

We borrowed a little nightlight. It didn't do much to the black all around it. I followed him up the stairs in a wobbly patch of light. When we got to my door I tried to push it open and I couldn't. Sam tried with his shoulder.

He said, "You're locked out."

I sat down with my back to the door and my bum on the scratchy doormat. I'd let the door shut behind me. The keys were inside.

Sam said maybe I should go back downstairs to Isabel's.

"No," I said.

He said, "You can't sleep at mine."

"I don't want to. I'll sleep here."

"OK," he said. "I'll go and borrow a blanket."

"You can't tell her," I said. "If you tell her I'll have to go. Her cocoa is *horrible*."

He said he didn't have a blanket to lend me and I said I didn't need one.

The wax in the nightlight was turning to water, sloshing about. The flame kept almost drowning.

"You can't sleep here," he said. "Isabel will kill me."

"My mum'll be back soon," I said. "She probably just went for a walk or something."

Then Sam said, "Did you leave a window open?"

"Maybe. Why?"

"I can climb in if you did."

"Climb in how?" I said.

He said he could go out of his window and up to mine.

"Is that dangerous?"

"It's no different to rock climbing."

I said, "Can you really climb a building in the dark. Is that even allowed?"

Sam smiled. "I've done it before. It's not that hard."

He said he was going to go down and find his torch and look out at my windows. He took two steps towards the stairs and started to disappear.

"Don't leave me by myself," I said.

"Well, come with me then," he said.

When we got to his floor, I heard Isabel's voice from downstairs. "She all right, Country?" she said.

Sam signalled for me to be quiet and he said, "Yeah, fine. She'll be asleep any minute."

"Where's that bloody woman got to do you think?" she said, meaning my mum.

Sam looked at me. "I don't know, Isabel. I'm going to bed now. Goodnight."

"I've got a good mind to report her to someone or other."

"Not tonight, Isabel."

"No, the phones are out. But I should though. I should phone someone tomorrow."

I wanted to say maybe there was a reason my mum was

out, an emergency or something. I wanted to say she wasn't a bloody woman. I wanted to say that Isabel should be nicer if she wanted to stay friends with me, and that if she told *anyone*, I would never, *ever* speak to her again.

But I had to keep my mouth shut or I'd get found out.

Sam opened his door and we crept in without a sound.

His room was the same size as ours, but tidier and weirdly empty. I thought it was just the darkness hiding things so when he found the torch I borrowed it and moved the beam around the room, looking for stuff. It was like nobody lived there. He had the smallest pile of clothes folded in one corner, a mattress by a window and a book or two. That was it.

"Where's all your stuff?" I whispered.

He'd opened the window at the front and he was trying to see out. He shrugged and took the torch into the kitchen. "It's all here," he said.

I pictured our flat with clothes everywhere and a pile of suitcases and everything falling over itself in the kitchen.

"I think the front windows are shut," he said. "I'll have a look at the back."

He opened the window in his kitchen and pointed the torch up. All I could see in the dark was his throat.

"That one's open," he said. "See?" And he pointed. It was a long way away.

"Is that our kitchen?" I said.

He was looking at the wall. He wasn't listening. He said, "I can use the drainpipe that goes between them. That's the quickest way to do it."

"All the way up there?" I said. It wasn't giving me a good feeling.

"I guess so."

"Maybe I should sleep on Isabel's sofa."

"I've lied to her now," he said. The circle of torchlight bounced while he climbed up on to the windowsill. "And you don't want to."

I didn't, he was right. Even more now I'd heard what she said when I wasn't supposed to be listening.

Sam gave me the torch before he put his top half outside. He was sitting on the windowsill and holding on to the edges. He leaned back to look up and I felt my stomach dropping. I pointed the torch out there for him, to be helpful. He looked into the light and screwed up his eyes.

"Point it up there," he said, nodding his head cos he wasn't letting go with his hands.

I put one arm out of the window next to him and aimed the torch. The bright circle of it travelled up the side of the building and turned the blackness back to bricks. "Please be careful!" I said.

"It's easy," he told me. "I just have to grab the pipe for a second, then there's a foothold there, Mick's windowsill, a bit more pipe and I'm up."

He pulled himself out and stood on the outside of his window. All I could see was his legs and his trainers. All I could think was that this was a really bad plan and he was going to fall and maybe die, just cos I wanted to be in my room.

"Shall we wait for my mum?" I said, but he didn't hear me. His legs were suddenly only in the top half of the window, and then one foot, and then nothing, just the black, black sky and the quiet flicker of candles in other people's houses.

I stood in his empty flat in the dark. I heard a noise above me and I shut my eyes. I imagined the whoosh of his falling body, the crump of him landing far below.

But it didn't come.

Instead I heard his voice and I shone the torch up and he was in, looking out of my kitchen down at me in his. "OK," he whispered. "You can come up."

I looked up out of the window, at the way he'd climbed, and then down at the ground. "Can you believe that?" I said to nobody in particular.

I made sure his door didn't close behind me.

I went as quietly as I could on the stairs. It was easy with a torch. Sam was standing at my door, holding the bag of candles.

I said, "That was really cool."

"Where are your matches? Have you got any?"

When I opened the loo door to find some, the light of the torch landed on Mum, fast asleep, curled up like a bug in the corner. At the same time, there was a pop in the hallway and the lights came back on. The sudden brightness made me blink and squint.

Mick was in there too, lying in the empty bath with all his clothes on. He made a groaning noise and opened his eyes. Mum opened hers too and then shut them again. She said, "What time is it?"

I was still holding the torch and its light looked weak and yellow in the white light of the bulb. I knew that Sam was behind me and I knew that he'd seen.

"Is she OK?" he said.

My smile felt weird on my face, like one of those cardboard ones you can hold with a lolly stick.

All I could think of to say was, "She wasn't out after all."

The Story of My Life
Part Three
by B Hoban

Mum met Uncle Paul at the Casino. She told Nancy he was on a roll cos the first things she noticed about him were his suit and his watch and his winter tan. Later she said the suit must've been borrowed and the watch and the tan were fakes. She says a lot worse things about him when she's been drinking, but I never minded Uncle Paul. He was nice to me and when he showed up I didn't have to be on my own any more, or hardly anyway, cos Mum stopped working again. He didn't like Mum going to work. I said that to Mum once, but never again cos she just gave me a list of reasons why he was the worst of them all.

Paul moved into Nancy's flat, even though it was only supposed to be girls in there. They spent most of their time in our bedroom. I made friends with the family downstairs, which was big and didn't mind me staying over. We could hear Paul and Mum through the ceiling, but from down there it was funny.

That family worried about me. I know because they told people when I was there, in that way that grown-ups talk about kids and pretend we can't hear them. Everyone in that family liked me. I was happy.

So when Mum said that we were moving to the seaside, just like that, I said I wasn't going. I sat in the corner of the hall where the wall met the stairs and I cried. Paul gave her this blank, cold look and said he'd be back in two hours to pick us up.

Mum shouted at me when he'd gone. She said I had no right to talk to Paul like that when he was jut trying to put a better roof over our heads. She said my friends would be glad to see the back of me cos I was there all the bloody time. She stuffed my clothes into bin bags and threw them at the front door while she was shouting.

I went downstairs to say goodbye, and thank you for having me, and sorry if I was there too much, but there was nobody home.

We lasted about five minutes in Brighton.

Paul left us and started going out with a nurse he met at

the dentist. He'd been having root canal work done, which sounds gruesome, but Mum said it was far less gross than eyeing someone up while you're doing it. She also said she wasn't that bothered. She said she'd had enough of him anyway and that he was starting to get fat.

We moved back to Nancy's cos Nancy was going away for a while.

It was better being just the two of us. About a week after we got there, Mum said to me, "God, you got tall!" like she hadn't been looking or something.

Ten (Sam)

We used to lose power at home all the time. It was never something that took you by surprise, not really. Everyone I knew had a stash of lamps and candles and torches and batteries. Everyone I knew could make a decent fire in the dark.

Later, after I'd climbed in Bohemia's window, I sat in my room in the dark. I suppose it was a welcome thing, to have been in proper blackness again. There was a hush I wasn't used to, like everything was holding its breath until the lights came back on. My fingers tingled from holding on to the bricks. My whole body had this quiet hum in the middle of it, like a tuning fork, like pure adrenaline.

I'd climbed up the side of Max's house a couple of times. Once for a dare and once to prove to my friends that I'd actually done it. Rock climbing was never really my thing at all. Rock climbing centres smell of sweat and other people's fear, and on a real rock everything takes too long, like putting up shelves. I'm too impatient. The dogs at Max's barked at me, but nobody paid them any attention because they barked at anything. They'd barked wolf.

The first time, they barked and yelped themselves crazy, and stood on their hind legs in their enclosure. I took a run up and grabbed the drainpipe a couple of feet above my head. It was a rough stone wall with plenty of good holes and lots of ivy. It was easier than the one I'd just done, not as high up.

I was never scared of the climbing. I was more scared of getting caught, of Max's Mum and Dad watching in the dark, their hands on the window, palms flat against the glass.

I couldn't get the sight of Cherry and Mick out of my head. The state of them slumped in the bathroom, half dressed, like corpses. And Bohemia, afraid and still smiling, pretending it was nothing.

She was alone in a way I'd never be.

I didn't want to see it. I was way out of my depth in that much aloneness. I was useless. So I left her there.

I shut the door behind me in my own empty room and I thought about phoning home. I imagined hearing it ring. I knew exactly where it was and exactly how it sounded. It's dark in there, in the centre of the house, with only the reflection of light on the walls from windows in other rooms. Even on a bright day the tiles on the floor are cold and outside sounds far away.

I thought about what Mum and Dad would be doing when the phone rang. Dad's hands covered in soil, his palms thick and dry with it, rich brown in his nails where there used to be white. He'd shout to Mum to pick up because he wouldn't get his boots off in time. Where would she be? Folding laundry, making a list, reading the newspaper with her glasses low on the bridge of her nose.

Neither of them would be passed out half naked on a bathroom floor.

It would mean something to them that the phone call was from me.

Mum and Dad moved away from London before I was born. They always said that city people who move to the country are never at home. Wherever they are, they miss the things they love about wherever they're not.

You fall in love with the spaces and the air, while you pine for the crowds and the movement.

You learn four hundred and fifty new shades of green, but everyone's skin is the same colour.

You crave the lights and the speed and the noise that when you get there are too bright and too fast and too loud.

Mum said that the things she missed most about the city were the strangers. All the people she travelled to work near, or negotiated busy streets around, or went to the cinema beside. All the people she didn't see the first time and never saw again. "They make up the landscape," she said. "You have no idea how precious they are until they're gone."

I liked the things about London they'd have wanted me to like. I loved how fast everything was and how changing.

I loved strangers and I especially loved being one.

I liked the fact that everything you needed was just there, around the next corner, at any time of day or night.

I liked that you could get pretty much anywhere just using your feet.

I liked graffiti and litter and the smell of eight different takeaways on any given street.

I liked the way people talked to each other, and the way they didn't talk to me.

I liked reading the same mortgage advert for seven stops on the Tube because nobody said you had to look at an actual person.

I liked that I didn't have to think about what I'd left behind and how much trouble I was in.

But at the same time, if I'd had the guts to ring, if I could have talked to them about coming from one place and living in another, here's what I would say.

These are the things a country person misses in the city:

The smell of air. And cow shit (honest). And clothes that have dried outside in the sun.

The soothing properties of the colour green.

The incessant whisper of trees.

The size of the sky.

That a river is never the same twice and is always a surprise in the morning.

How loud birds can actually be.

That what you know is there, however much you didn't know it when you had the chance.

These are the things that were glowing and flashing and beeping and whirring when everyone woke up the next morning. I only know because Steve did a tour of the place, counting all the appliances. He came to the door, banged on it like the police, started talking before I got it open, walked in before I asked him. He was this ball of energy and it was early.

"What are you doing?" I said when he started opening things in the kitchen, sniffing the milk.

"I was going to make you some coffee."

"I don't drink coffee."

He looked at me like this was a possibility he had never in all his life considered. "I can't even open my eyes without coffee," he said.

He'd made a list and he showed it to me. He read it out loud while I tried to wake up.

One amp for an electric guitar (Steve's), four stereos, three iPods (on charge), one computer, two laptops, three modems, three telephones, two answer machines, two mobiles (on charge), two TVs, one fish tank (Mick's), two microwaves, four ovens and their timers, four radios, two alarm clocks, two fridge freezers, one boiler, one electric blanket (Isabel's), eight lamps and one portable sunbed (Steve's).

It was only one house. He said it didn't even include the flat where Cherry and the girl lived because they wouldn't let him in. He couldn't believe there had to be that much plugged in. He said we had to do something about how much power we were wasting.

He said, "I don't know where to start."

Then he poked around in my room. "Haven't you got anything electric?" he said. "Not even a radio?"

I shook my head. "Not here," I said.

While he was talking, I thought again about how the quiet

and dark of the power cut had reminded me of home. Black at night, every night. It made me remember that the city was built on the same land I was used to. Underneath the streets somewhere were the same soil and rocks and stretches of water. With the power, everything came back on in our one house and all the countless other houses around it, and you could forget about the underneath again.

"Imagine," I said, "how easily it might just turn back to the land if a power cut lasted forever, if nothing ever switched back on again."

"What are you on about?" Steve said, looking up from his list.

"About everything being the same underneath, however you try to disguise it," I said.

It was the most I'd ever said to him. I don't think he was that impressed.

The Story of My Life
Part Four
by B Hoban

After Paul, Mum met Ray and I wish she hadn't. Ray wasn't very nice to her, or me, or even Nancy whose house he was always in. In the end, Nancy and Mum had a big fight and she made us leave. Nancy said to me she was really sorry but there was nothing more she could do. I didn't like the sound of her saying that.

Ray had a nearly empty flat that was full of people all the time. I didn't even bother unpacking my Mary Poppins bag there cos all my good stuff would've got broken. Mum and Ray slept a lot and couldn't ever be bothered to move, and I played with the kids in the downstairs playground, until their mums found out what number flat I came from and then they weren't allowed to play with me any more.

When they weren't sleeping, Mum and Ray were fighting

and she was unhappy all of the time. And then one day Ray was gone and we were just some of the people in his horrible flat. I went back to Nancy and said please would she get Mum out of there. And Nancy did, and she got Mum a job with Mr Thing, and she said that was the last thing she was ever doing.

She said she was washing her hands of us. And she meant it.

I wish Ray had vanished into thin air, but he hadn't, and even though we didn't see him all the time like we used to, whenever Mum saw him, or even thought about him, I could tell, and it gave me a scared feeling, right in the middle. He was bad for her, like sweets and smoking and fried Mars bars and not enough sleep.

Eleven (Bohemia)

When I woke up I stayed in my tent and I ate a whole packet of Pink Panther biscuits. They make your mouth *really* dry, especially if you eat a load of them. I had to get up for a drink and to go to the loo. I was busting. I had that feeling when you wish someone else could go for you, but they never can. When I got back into bed it was all prickly with pink sawdust and I had to get it all out, and that was it then, I was up.

There was a knock on the door right when I was walking past it. It made me jump and I spilled water all down myself. It was a serious knock, like ONE-TWO-THREE and it made me think of police and people with clipboards, like straightaway. I sucked the water off my arm and I didn't say anything. ONE-TWO-THREE it went again. I stayed totally still cos I thought if I moved they might hear me.

Maybe Isabel phoned the people like she said she would. I was scared it was them.

Then this voice said, "Hello?" and it didn't sound like clipboards at all. It sounded more like someone with messy hair, dressed in a tracksuit with bare feet. It sounded like Steve. I wished we had one of those things you see in films, like a special glass hole in your door so you can see who's knocking. I tried to look through the keyhole, but it was too small and low down and full of fluff to be useful.

"Hello," it said again. "Anybody in there?"

It was probably Steve, but with no spyhole how could I be sure?

"Suit yourself," it said, and then the bare feet were on the stairs and he knocked lower down and I started breathing again.

Mum came out of the loo looking folded and angry. I don't know if Mick was still in there and I didn't ask. I put the bed away cos I was sick of looking at it. We didn't have a dustpan and brush to sweep up the crumbs so I blew most of them under the sofa. It was a bit crunchy under my feet so I put some socks and shoes on and it made sense to get the rest of me dressed as well.

"What are you doing today?" I said when she came back from the kitchen.

She was still just in her underwear. She didn't answer me.

"I need some clean clothes," I said.

She said, "Sorry, Bo."

I didn't know if she was talking about the laundry or about crashing out in the bathroom with beard-face. "Don't be," I said, but I didn't mean it.

Then I told her about the power cut and Sam climbing in everything.

"God, we didn't hear any of that," she said.

I went to the fridge and poured all the milk that was left into a cup and I didn't leave any for her, not even a drop for some tea. "Nope," I said. "You didn't."

"I have to go out later," she said.

"Where you going?"

"See some friends."

"Who?"

"You don't know them."

"When will you be back?"

She put her head in her hands and she groaned her morning groan, and she said, "Bo, lighten up. You're not my mum."

I glared at her when she said that, and I know I looked stupid standing there in my too-small clothes and my dirty hair, but that was her fault. "Yes, Cherry, I know," I said. "But you *are* mine."

And then I told her what Isabel said last night, the thing I wasn't supposed to hear, about telling someone, about reporting Cherry to the authorities for not looking after me properly and always being out and out of her head. I laid it on pretty thick. I probably made it sound *much* worse than it was really.

I shouldn't have done that.

Mum just sat there in her bra and knickers, with her bare legs folded underneath her and her feet all dirty and her tummy creased like a crocodile's tail and her mouth open.

I left her there and I went to see Sam.

I said, "It's me, Bohemia," at the same time as knocking, and I knocked gently so I didn't make him jump.

"What do you want?" he said. He didn't even open the door.

"Can you get my mum a job?" I said.

"God. I don't know. Doubt it."

I didn't know what else to say and I hadn't even meant to say that straightaway. I just stood there looking at the line on my side of the door where his black floor met the squishy old hall carpet.

"Anything else?"

"No," I said.

I counted to ten in my head and I didn't go away even though I know he wanted me to. Then he asked me if my mum was all right.

"No," I said.

"What's the matter with her?"

"Everything."

Sam opened the door then. We both looked at his big feet. He didn't have any shoes on.

"Can we go out?" I said.

"I don't think so."

"Please, Sam, just for a minute."

"Where do you want to go?"

"Wherever you like," I said.

"I've got to go to work," he said.

I had to beg and beg.

He put some shoes on and we went downstairs and outside. We didn't see anyone. It was cold and my arms were too long for my coat. They stuck way out of the sleeves and every time I tried to pull them down things got too tight across my shoulders.

"I've grown," I said.

Sam was really tall, but his coat looked fine on him. I asked him if he'd stopped growing. He looked at his hands as if he'd be able to tell. "I don't think so," he said.

"But you're enormous."

"My dad's six foot four," he said.

I said I wondered if my dad was tall. "I'll have to wait until

I stop growing to find out. If I'm really tall then maybe he is."

"Is it your dad who's got your red hair?"

"I don't know," I said. "I've never seen him."

"Not a photo or anything?"

"No."

"Well, you should ask Cherry where it comes from."

"What?"

"Your hair." It's what I noticed about you the first time I saw you," he said. "I remembered you because of your red hair."

I made a face. "I hate it."

"Don't be mad,' he said. "It's great. You'll like it when you're older."

"I'll dye it when I'm older," I said.

"Don't do that."

"Why not?"

We were walking past the Tube and he asked me if I'd ever been to the National Gallery.

"The what?"

"Trafalgar Square. You know, Nelson's Column, sculptures, fountains, National Gallery?"

"Don't think so."

"Me neither and I always wanted to."

"So let's go," I said.

I asked him why he'd thought of it. He said he'd heard

there were loads of beautiful ladies in there with hair like mine. He said we should see them.

"What about your work?" I said.

"I was lying. I start at seven. We've got ages."

Sam was *funny* on the Tube. As if he had to think harder than anyone else about where to put his ticket and which way he was going, stuff like that.

"It's like you're from another planet," I said.

"I thought I was heart-breakingly cool," he said, and I laughed some more cos he so wasn't.

"Mornington Crescent!" he said, like that was something. We'd only gone one stop.

"What?"

"My mum listens to it on the radio. It's a game that doesn't make any sense."

I said, "It's at the bottom of the High Street."

"Well, I know that. But it's this game and she laughs out loud, and she doesn't even know why."

He stopped talking then and I watched him cos I knew he was thinking about his mum. It must be a nice picture to have of someone in your mind, them laughing their head off at the radio.

Trafalgar Square was huge and it had fountains and everything.

I'd been past it on the bus loads of times, but I'd never stood in the middle and seen how huge and fancy it actually was. Everything was this pale golden colour, the floor and the buildings and stuff, like they got cleaned in the night while everyone was asleep.

The National Gallery was free, except for this big see-through box of money that you could put what you wanted in. Some people had put 2p's and some had put five pound notes, and there were buttons and bits of pocket fluff in there too, maybe from people who thought the pictures weren't up to much.

I liked them. I really did. There were so many to look at I thought my head might fill up with pictures and have no room for anything else.

The women with the red hair like mine were beautiful and draped over sofas like they had nothing else to do with their time. After a bit they looked all the same, but there was a wrinkly old lady I liked. From far away she looked like an actual photograph. Then when you got close, like you would to a real old lady, her skin was pink and green and yellow and purple and all the colours you could think of, and it was obvious somebody had done it with a brush. Her eyes had lots of things to say, more than the bored girls on the sofas. I looked at her for a long time.

I put half my money in the box on the way out. I would've put in more, but I wanted a sandwich.

We walked to the river and the tide was out, so we climbed down in the stones and the rubble and stuff. Sam picked up a piece of old plate and gave it to me. It was about the size of a 10p with two leaves on it. He said they were ivy. They might've been green once, but now they were all faded and blue. I held on to it. It was smooth under my thumb. We had to watch where we walked. There were chunks of old wall and rusted bars and bits of glass everywhere.

"You all right?" I said and he nodded.

He said, "You?"

I said my mum made me sad. It was the first time I said it out loud to anyone ever and it made me want to sit down and cry.

Sam said he thought my mum needed some help and I said I was doing my best. "Not from you," he said.

I didn't say anything to that.

"Did you run away, really?" I said, and he frowned at me and shook his head. I asked him, wasn't that what Isabel said? "You know, that nobody knows you're here."

"She doesn't know that for sure."

"Yeah, but it's true though, isn't it?"

He laughed, like an out blow of breath, and he didn't answer.

"I ran away once," I said. "I didn't get as far as you."

"Where did you go?"

"I got to the station, but I didn't have any money."

I was looking at the tiny cracked patterns on the bit of plate he gave me. I was picking at them with my finger.

"What did you do?"

"I walked home."

"Did you leave a note?"

"Course."

"And what did Cherry do when you got back?"

"Oh, she didn't notice," I said. "She thought I was in my room the whole time."

He looked at me then and put his hand out and messed up my hair. "What about the note? Didn't she see that?"

"It fell down the back of the cupboard. I got it out later."

Sam looked at me and I looked at the grey soupy water. "Did you leave a note?" I said.

"No."

"Why not?"

"Because I didn't know what to say."

"That's bad. You should leave a note."

"Why?"

"So people know you're going and stuff. So they don't think you got kidnapped or fell down a hole."

"Well, I didn't leave one," he said. "I fell down a hole. I didn't think anyone would mind."

"Why did you go?"

"Why did *you* go?"

"I asked first," I said.

Sam said he asked second and then neither of us said anything. He took the bit of plate out of my hand and stared at it.

"I went home after half an hour," I said. "You're still missing."

He didn't look at me or the river or anything. He just carried on picking at the bit of smashed plate.

"Can we not talk about it?" he said.

When I got home there was a pile of clean clothes for me on the sofa, folded up and nice-smelling. Mum had her hair tied back and no make-up and comfy clothes. She was smiling like she'd done something amazing and everybody had to celebrate. I wanted to smile back, but I was still cross.

I picked up the first few shirts and dropped them on the floor on purpose. "I can't wear those," I said. "They're way too small."

Mum's smile cracked and she grabbed her keys off the side, and she said, "Right, I'm going to go and have words with that cow downstairs."

"What?" I said, and I wanted to take what I'd just done away again. I wanted to walk in and hug her and say thanks for washing my stuff.

"That old woman on the ground floor," Mum said. "The one who reckons she's telling the social."

"Don't do that," I said.

"Why not?" Mum yelled at me.

"She didn't call, did she," I said. "They didn't come."

"I'm not having you judging me thanks to *her*," she said. "I'm not scared of an old woman."

I tried to stop her. I held on to her arm and I said please like a hundred times, but once my mum's decided she wants to have it out with someone that's usually kind of it.

I put my hands over my ears and sang so I wouldn't have to listen to the shouting.

Steve came up from the basement. I saw him through the window. Mick came out of his flat and shot down the stairs so fast he bounced off the walls. He sounded like a box falling. I could hear them talking, trying to stop Isabel and my mum from tearing each other apart.

I was glad Sam was at work so he didn't have to hear it.

When the front door slammed, I looked out of the window again. It was Mick and my mum. He had his arm around her and she didn't have anything on her feet. They just stood really close together in the street talking and I watched them through the glass, but I couldn't hear what they said.

Isabel wasn't saying anything any more. I couldn't hear her.

I was ashamed to be the cause of all that commotion.

I should have just kept my mouth shut.

Twelve (Sam)

I had no idea how much Isabel knew until she started talking. I was in her kitchen, fixing a cupboard door that had eaten itself around the hinges. Don't ask me how she'd persuaded me to do it. She said Steve was out. I think it was a trick to get me down there. She probably ate the cupboard herself.

Bohemia was in the park with Doormat again. We watched them walk off together, her chatting away to him like he was anyone, like he understood every word.

"How was she yesterday?" she said.

"Oh, you know," I said. "Talkative."

"Poor you," she said. "You come here like a hermit on a vow of silence and you get adopted by a ten-year-old with verbal diarrhoea."

Isabel said she'd had a fight with Cherry. She said, "When that girl is angry, she is *not* a pretty sight."

"Bet you are though," I said.

I had my head in the cupboard. I was taking off the door. My voice bounced off the walls and came straight back at me. I thought about Bohemia in the park with the dog, chatting away, with her skinny little limbs and her Pringles lunches and her tired eyes and her smile. I think we both did. "Poor kid," I said.

She said, "That makes two of you."

"I'm all right."

"Don't be ridiculous."

"I am, Isabel. And I'm hardly a kid."

"You're somebody's kid," she said.

I pulled a face at her inside the cupboard. She didn't see me.

"How long are you going to keep it up?" she said. "I lie awake at night worrying about you, as well you know."

"Don't bother," I said. "I'm not exactly living on the streets. And I *have* got a job."

"You're doing very well," she said. "Your loved ones would be so proud of you if they knew you were alive."

"Don't do that," I said.

"Don't do what?"

I breathed out hard and I didn't say anything.

"Don't act all disappointed in me," she said. "I'm only trying to help."

"You know nothing about me," I said. "Nothing at all."

"Well, that's my point exactly."

"Yes," I said. "And that's why I moved."

"To the wrong house," she said.

I screwed the cupboard door back on and I swept the sawdust off the counter with one hand into the other. "That's done," I said.

"Thank you."

I started walking to the door.

"You have to call them," she said. "Or write to them even. You have to tell them you're alive."

"Isabel, *please* stay out of it."

"I'm sorry, Sam, but if you don't call them then I will."

I turned back to her. She was at the other end of the hallway, this small, determined, meddling old woman.

"Why would you do that?"

"Because they're worried."

"You sure about that, are you?"

"Yes, I am."

"You don't have their number," I said. "How are you going to call?"

"Well, I'll find it."

"How? I'm not just going to tell you it because you let me walk your dog. I'm not Bohemia. I'm not some motherless little kid who doesn't know what you're up to."

"Right now you are."

I put my head in my hands and I asked her really nicely. "Isabel, leave me alone, OK? I mean it."

She wouldn't let up. "Sam Cassidy," she said. "Born what, 1991? 1992?"

I wanted to walk away. "So? I won't be the only one."

"Are you the only Sam Cassidy that went to Highfield School?"

This cold, floorless place suddenly opened up inside me.

"How do you know that?" I said.

"It's hell for your mum and dad," she said. "How long have you been gone?"

"Stop it!" I shouted.

"They'll be worried sick. Life doesn't just carry on for the people you leave behind you know."

"You don't know anything," I said.

"It was on your T-shirt."

"What was?"

"The night I got locked out and you let me in, half asleep. Highfield School was on your T-shirt." She laughed at me. "If you're going to disappear without a trace, you don't usually bring your school uniform with you."

"Why are you doing this to me?" I said.

Isabel shook her head. "Don't be such a child, Sam. I just want to help you do the right thing."

I felt lead-heavy, exhausted. "Why do they need to know where I am?" I said.

"Why do you think?"

"Want to know what I think? I think they're better off."

She asked me if I really meant it, if that's what I believed. "Why are you talking like that?" she said.

"You don't know what I've done."

"So tell me."

I shouted at her then. I told her no. I said, "Nobody here knows what I've done."

Isn't that why I moved here in the first place?

Thirteen (Bohemia)

I waited for Mum as long as I could, but I think she stayed at Mick's that night cos she didn't come home. She was making me pay for being cross with her. I did cleaning so she'd be pleased with me and know I was sorry. I shook the sheets and I cleaned the kitchen, then the loo, and then I ran a big bath with bubbles like Mum does. I washed everything, even my hair, now that I had to like it and everything. I had to use washing up liquid cos we'd run out of everything else. It made my hair squeak, but it didn't fall out or anything so that was OK. I made a bra top out of bubbles and just lay there like a mermaid. It was luxury.

Isabel knocked on the door and so did Steve, but I was in the water both times, watching my fingers go like raisins, powerless to get out and save them. "I'm in the bath," I said, and I made lots of splashing noises.

Isabel said did I want to come down for my tea.

Steve wanted to talk to Mum. He said it was a rent thing. I really hoped he wouldn't throw us out for fighting with Isabel.

I said, "Is it late?" and he said "Is what late?"

"The rent?"

"Oh. No, it's fine. I just wanted to give her a receipt."

"That's a relief," I said. I held my breath and let go with my feet so my head went under. I didn't hear what he said next or when he went away.

After that I lay around in bed for ages, drawing pictures, and she still didn't come. I must have fallen asleep waiting.

The next day I played with Doormat, throwing his ruined ball for him down the steps. Isabel said I'd give him a heart attack, making him run up and down like that, cos he was just an old man, and I was worried until she said she was only joking. I watched TV in her house for ages. Then Sam came down to fix something and I had to take Doormat across to the park. I didn't really want to, but Isabel kept nodding and pointing like I didn't really have a choice. When I got back we made cakes in paper cases and she said they were so good we should eat them all and not tell anyone.

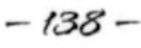

We sat at the kitchen table with our mouths full of cake.

"Where's Sam?" I said. "Shouldn't we save him one?"

"He's gone out," she said. "He's angry with me."

"Why?"

"Because I'm an interfering old woman."

"He's not angry," I said. "He misses Max."

"Who's Max?"

"His friend. He knows everything about ants. Sam told me about him."

"What did Sam tell you?"

I asked her did she know that ants are like farmers. "They don't farm cows, *obviously*, cos cows are too big, but they farm these little bugs called aphids. They have herds of them and they milk them and *everything*."

"Is that true?" she said.

"Yep."

"Well I never. What else did Sam tell you?"

"He said that ants weigh more than people if you add them all up, but I don't believe him. He told me about this thing he saw where they poured concrete into an ant place and then ex-ca-somethinged it, like dug it up but really gently, with brushes, and it looked like something from the future, with all these pods and runways and stuff."

"Colony," Isabel said. "An ant place is called a colony."

"OK."

I put a cake to one side for Sam. I said I was really sorry about the fight she'd had with my mum.

Isabel shrugged in that way that means you're pretending you don't care, but you're still cross. She said, "Everyone's falling out with me at once."

"I'm not," I said, and she squeezed my hand across the table and called me dear.

I wanted to say it was my fault, the fight, cos I'd heard what she said on the stairs when I was supposed to be in bed. I wanted to, but I didn't want me and Sam to get in trouble for the climbing up the building thing, and then anyway she changed the subject and asked me again why I didn't go to school, a clever girl like me.

"I don't know," I said, cos Mum wasn't there to ask.

"Why don't you know?" she said.

"I don't know."

"Well, think about it."

I actually did.

Later, I wanted to see Sam. I went to find him. He wasn't in his room so I waited. I didn't mean anything by it.

He ignored me when he got home. I thought he hadn't seen me so I said "Hello" or something, and he opened the door and I walked in under his arm. I could see where he'd been sitting before he went to work, right by the window. There was a folded up jumper there, like a cushion, and a mug with cold tea in the bottom.

"What are you doing?" he said.

"Nothing much."

"Why are you doing it outside my room?"

"Isabel said you're cross with her."

"I am."

"What for?"

"For being an interfering old woman."

"That's what she said."

"Good."

I started breathing on the window and drawing hearts in it. "What did she do?"

"She won't mind her own business. She's into everybody's secrets."

I said I thought she was nice, trying to be helpful all the time.

Sam looked down at me. He looked angrier than I'd ever seen him. "Where's your mum, Bohemia?" he said.

I breathed on the window again. "She popped out."

"How long for?"

"Don't know."

I was trying to draw a house without taking my finger off

the window. It's like a square with a cross in it and a triangle roof, and I know it's possible, I just couldn't remember how to start. "She thinks I should go to school," I said.

He was frowning out of the window. "Who? Isabel?"

"Yes."

"See? What's it got to do with her?"

"I think it's nice that she wants me to."

I asked him if he liked school and he said it was all right. I asked him what his best subjects were and he said, "Maths and football," which was just weird.

I said, "What colour was your uniform?"

"Blue."

"How many people in your class?"

"I don't want to play now," he said.

"Did you have lots and lots and lots of friends?"

He sighed. "I had a few."

I said, "Do you think you'll go back ever?"

Sam growled and put his head in his hands and said, "I don't know, Bohemia. God, you're as bad as her. Are you working together or something?"

I said I was just asking. He didn't look at me or smile or anything.

I said, "I just wanted to know about school. I haven't been for ages and I don't know what it's like. I don't know anyone the same age as me and I wouldn't want to get picked on for being stupid or ginger or new. I wanted you to help me. I didn't want to know your stupid secrets."

I picked up a book that was by his bed. I tried to turn on his mobile phone. Sam said mean things then.

He told me to leave his stuff alone.

He said he was the last person I should be asking.

He told me to go and talk to someone who was interested.

He said it wasn't his fault my mum was a drunk and a junkie and a loser.

He said he couldn't look after me any more.

He said, "Why does Cherry forget to come home, Bohemia? Is it because you *won't stop bloody talking*?"

Boy, was he going to regret that in the morning.

Fourteen (Sam)

I felt bad as soon as she was gone. Of course I did. She stood by the door and she had her arms folded across her chest like she was hugging herself, I suppose because nobody else would. She said she was going now. She said she thought I was her friend, but clearly she was wrong. She said she was very sorry to have made such a mistake.

She didn't say it like that. Bohemia Hoban has a foul mouth.

I felt bad about it as soon as she left. I should have gone after her and made it better, but I didn't. I'm an idiot.

I lay on my mattress without taking my shoes off. I stared at the sky. I tried to sleep.

I thought about what a bad person I was and I wondered

when that had actually happened and why it took so long for me to notice.

I slept that kind of sleep where you think you're still awake the whole time. I woke up in the dark out of a dream I couldn't remember, except I knew it was about Max. The dream got me up and out to the phone box. It wasn't night and it wasn't morning. I couldn't decide. I actually thought I was going to phone him. I'm not sure when I realised that it wasn't going to happen – somewhere between being out on the pavement and picking up the receiver. I put it down and stood there in the piss stink, looking out and seeing nothing.

So the next day it was me, for once, banging on Bohemia's door at some hideous hour of the morning. I said, "Bohemia, come on! I'm sorry."

No answer, just the movement of sheets.

"Really, I mean it."

"I mean I *didn't* mean it," I said. "The stuff I said yesterday. I was just pissed off, that's all. Not at you."

The door opened and Cherry's delicate, haggard face filled the gap. "That's a weight off," she said.

"Where's Bohemia?" I said.

"I dunno," she said. "I thought she was with one of you."

"Are you sure she's not there?" I said. "Not asleep in the bathroom or something?"

"Who the hell is that?" Mick's voice growled from somewhere inside. "What's the time, for Christ's sake?"

"She's not here," Cherry said. "Go away."

I went down to Isabel's. I didn't have to knock to get her out of bed. She was already up, wiping the front door with an old tea towel. "It's vinegar before you ask," she said.

"What is?"

"The smell. I've been cleaning my windows."

I asked her what time she got up in the morning.

"I couldn't sleep."

"Why not?"

She shrugged her shoulders and carried on rubbing the paintwork off. "I'm sorry about yesterday," she said.

"Me too."

She smiled. "I didn't mean anything by it," she said. "I'd never phone them really. I never would."

"OK."

"I wrote you a note," she said. "I was deciding whether to deliver it."

"Where is it?"

"On the kitchen table."

"Can I read it?"

She shrugged and rubbed extra hard at some part of the doorknob. "I'd rather you didn't."

"Is Bohemia with you?" I said.

"No. I'm sure she's upstairs, sleeping like a baby. It's six-thirty, Sam."

"I know," I said. "I woke Cherry up."

"Ha! Good." She winked at me.

"Bohemia's not there," I said.

"Bet she is."

"Mick's there," I said.

Isabel rolled her eyes and clucked her tongue. "Right pair of lovebirds."

"It doesn't feel right, Isabel. She's not here."

"That woman couldn't find her own nose before ten in the morning. Go and look yourself."

I went back upstairs and got Cherry out of bed again. She was more bothered by that than the idea her daughter might have gone somewhere in the middle of the night.

"What time did you get home?" I said.

"How do I know?"

Her make-up had dropped while she was sleeping. It filled the slipping, puffy skin beneath her eyes with pockmarks of shadow and glitter.

"Well. Was it dark?" I said. "Were the birds singing? Were there people about and were they going home or going to work?"

"Is that you *again*?" Mick shouted.

"It was dark," she said with her eyes closed and her head leaning on the door. "I dropped my keys in the street and I had to use my lighter to find them."

"Where did you go?" I asked her.

"What's it to you?"

"It's nothing to me at all. Can I come in?"

She laughed. "Help yourself, darling. The more the merrier."

The sheets from the sofa bed were all over the floor. The room smelled like an ashtray.

Bohemia wasn't there.

I went back down to Isabel. I said, "Do you think she's run away?"

The wrinkles on her face were deep, like they'd been drawn in with a pencil, the ditches of her skin filled with shadow. "Why would she do that?" she said.

"I don't know. Maybe she's bored of her millionaire lifestyle."

"Well, where would she go?"

"I have no idea."

We searched the house then. We knocked at Steve's. We got Mick to open his place. We looked in the yard. Isabel even checked in Doormat's basket.

Bohemia was gone.

Everyone kept making suggestions.

Maybe she was at the shops.

Or gone for a walk.

Or hiding somewhere we hadn't thought to look yet, waiting for us to find her.

Maybe she'd be back any minute.

Maybe she was upstairs fast asleep after all.

"She'll be pleased somebody's noticed," I said, but none of them knew what I was talking about.

Even then, when everyone was being careful not to panic, I knew she'd gone.

I was worried she'd gone because of me.

Fifteen (Bohemia)

I wish I could've taken Doormat with me. All the adventures I've seen where kids run away and dice with danger, they've always got some clever dog on their side. Not that Doormat was probably all that clever, and he would've had to be carried cos his legs are useless. But at least he'd have kept me warm at night cos it was bloody cold some of the time. And I couldn't have taken him without asking. And he would've probably barked at me when I was hiding somewhere at a crucial moment, and I would've got caught. And I didn't want *anyone* to know.

I stole the money from Sam's room. I honestly didn't mean to. It was inside a book. I meant to steal that. He was being horrible to me at the time so I didn't feel bad about it. I just stuffed it up my jumper when he was glaring out the window and saying stuff about my mum, and telling me he didn't want to be my friend any more or something. When I got back to my room, all this money fell out and that's when I knew what to do.

I didn't count it. I put it in my sock. It had surprisingly sharp edges.

I put my warmest and waterproofest clothes on. I took Cherry's anorak cos it was big enough to keep me dry all over. I filled her pockets with the food that was left over in the kitchen until I was heavy with it. Maybe it was a good thing I wasn't taking Doormat after all. Knowing how greedy that dog is, he'd probably have eaten me alive, like a walking snack.

I didn't leave a note. That was on purpose. Let Sam see how *that* feels.

I managed to get past Isabel's door, but I nearly got caught as soon as I left the house. I shut the door without even a click, and I put my hood up and my head down and I walked to the end of the street. I was going to turn left when I got there and I was checking the road for cars, and right in front of me, in the stinky phone box, was Sam. I looked straight at him and for a second I swear he looked back at me, and then I hid my face and held my breath and kept on walking. I waited for him to shout out my name, but he didn't. I was happy and a bit disappointed at the same time.

I don't know what he was doing there. He wasn't even on the phone. He was just staring.

You can't really travel on public transport in the middle of the night when you're a kid cos people would ask questions on the night bus. It would've taken me less than half an hour to get to Victoria if I'd waited until later. But if I'd waited, I might not have done it. So that's why I was walking there at that time in the morning, with no dog for company and my mum's coat filled with food.

It's one of the things me and Mum always did together – walk everywhere cos there was never any money to spare. Isabel said that I never learned anything at home, but she's wrong cos I got really good at knowing how to get places and I bet that's worth a load more than your seven times table in the real world. I wanted to remember to tell her that when I saw her again.

I stayed close to walls and tried not to get noticed, and mostly it worked. I went round the Town Hall at the bottom of the High Street and down Hampstead Road. Past the old cigarette factory that Isabel said they painted to look like Egypt in Las Vegas, past the big flats that went on for streets and streets and one of them was Ray's, past the funny bar that was pretending to be in *Bugsy Malone*. There were people working already in the shops opposite the big glass buildings, stacking shelves like Sam did, and I didn't want them to see me so I went round the back, like three sides of a square, and crossed the road to the round end of Portland Place. It was still dark, as dark as it gets anyway. I know that now.

There weren't many people around. I thought I saw a little old lady shuffling along on the other side of the road, but it was me in my mum's coat, reflected in a window. It made me laugh. At least if anyone came up to me, I could hide my face and pretend to be a mad old battleaxe.

That's what Mum said to me once. "If you're out at night on your own and you want to make sure you're safe, act madder than the next person and they'll stay away from you."

So I was a cross between Isabel and my mum, walking along, with Sam's money in my sock and his book getting covered in food in my pocket.

I crossed over Oxford Street where you normally get herded from one side to the other. There weren't any policemen with megaphones and there wasn't even that man who wears the blackboard about how we're all going to die and rot in hell unless we give up eating cheeseburgers. I wondered what happened to him, where he went at night and if he had a wife that wore a blackboard too, so they could write messages to each other instead of talking.

There was someone sitting on top of the paper stand and I didn't notice them until it was too late cos I was looking at the headline. Sam told me that in the countryside those things were always really silly, like SWIMMING POOL PLAN HOLDS WATER and ANGER OVER GYPSY DROPPINGS. But this one was talking about someone being stabbed on their birthday, and then the person I hadn't noticed hopped down behind me quite close and started walking.

I felt a bit sick. I went very hot and very cold inside my coat. I didn't want any trouble cos I wouldn't know what to do with it. I'm only ten, for God's sake.

The footsteps asked me for a cigarette and I didn't look round, I just shook my head. Then he asked me for a pound for bus fare so I felt around in my pocket and offered him a Mars bar.

"What's that?"

I kept my face buried and tried to sound old and gruff. "It's a Mars bar," I said.

I looked up quickly while he was taking it. He wasn't very old. He had really bad skin and holes in his trainers. I hoped he wasn't anything to be afraid of. I didn't know if I should carry on trying to be an old lady or just show him my face. I didn't know which one of me he'd want to hurt less.

"Can I go now?" I said, trying to speed up a bit and not trip on the coat.

"Haven't you got any money?"

I could feel it in my sock, creasing against my leg with every step. "Nope. Sorry. I just gave you my breakfast."

He slowed down and I knew then that he wasn't going to do anything. And of course I was glad. How could I show them at Georgiana Street what I could do all by myself if I got kidnapped outside Topshop?

I ran into a side street ahead of him and hid in a doorway until he'd gone past, just in case. He threw the wrapper on to the pavement.

It was getting lighter when I got to St James's Park. It was empty apart from the pigeons who dived in and landed at my feet if I as much as rustled my crisp packet. I scattered the crumbs when the bag was empty and they fought over them with their fish eyes still looking at me, and their stabbing little heads.

It was just after six o'clock when I got to the coach station. I know cos there's an enormous clock there – you can't miss it. I undid my coat and wrapped it into a sort of a parcel cos I wasn't allowed to look like a crazy old lady in here, no way. I had to look like a little girl who'd just been sent on an errand by her mum, which was going to be easy when the station was full of other kids doing the same thing, but right now was hard cos there were twelve men and four old ladies in it. I sat on a chair, on my coat, and I waited. I think I slept, but not for long.

When it was more crowded and safe to move about, I looked at a map. And when I'd worked out where to go, I bought a ticket and I said thank you to Sam in my head.

I found a family that was going where I was going and sort of attached myself to them, not enough for them to notice, but enough for the ticket lady to think we were together. Every time I tried to smile at the littlest kid and look like I belonged, she stuck her tongue out and grabbed hold of her mum's arm.

"It's all right," I wanted to say. "I'm not staying. I'm on an important misson."

On the coach I sat down on my coat again, next to an old man who thought my mum was behind me. He was fast asleep after about eight minutes anyway. It smelled of bleach in there, and the dust heating up on the backs of the seats, and someone's sausage sandwich. I wished I'd bought a bottle of water in the station cos I was dying of thirst.

The lady at the front pointed out the toilet we could all smell and wished us a pleasant journey. She looked like she'd rather be at home in bed. She had the microphone right up against her lips so all the words she said were like little bomb blasts. I covered my ears with my hands and she glared at me, so I pretended to be asleep for the first bit of the journey so she wouldn't notice me. I closed my eyes and I thought about everyone.

I thought about my dad, whoever he might be, and what things we were both good at, thanks to him.

I thought about my mum and how I hoped she was home when I got back and how I hoped she was different.

I thought about Isabel, who actually was the nosiest and the kindest and the wrinkliest person I knew, apart from Steve who was maybe wrinklier. And I thought about Steve too and how nice he was to me always.

And last I thought about Sam and how lovely he was, and how sad, and how I was doing this just to show him.

It's quite stressful being on an adventure. You make it so far and then you realise you really *can't* mess it up cos everything's depending on it.

Sixteen (Sam)

How do you know when a kid who spends most of her time out and about on her own is really missing? When do you tell someone about it?

Isabel said we had to wait. She said we couldn't call the police straightaway because Bohemia hadn't been gone long enough. She said they'd ask all kinds of awkward questions. She said we'd have to get Cherry in a cold shower and tell her what to say or things would get worse for Bohemia and it would be our fault.

"Worse than what?" I said.

Isabel told me not to panic. She said, "I bet you she'll be back now, any minute, with something unsuitable for breakfast. She'll get an earful from me when she is." She blew on her coffee, the skin around her mouth corrugated like the paper cake cases on the kitchen table.

But Isabel was wrong for once, the one time I wanted her to be right. Bohemia didn't come back, with her gravestone smile and her instant affection and her wittering on.

"I'll go and look in a few places," I said.

"Good idea," Isabel said, frowning at her hands. "Keep yourself busy."

I walked where we walked with Doormat. I went to the park and into the woods where we'd seen the ants, all gone now, and into the playground where I know she'd have gone if she'd had anyone her age to play with. I checked the tubes in the climbing frame train. I could picture her there as I walked towards them. I could see her, fast asleep, wrapped up in a coat. I wanted to picture her coming back from the station like she'd told me, with no money, except this time everybody had noticed.

I went to the shop, just in case she was there, and I walked up and down the High Street, round the back, over and over, hoping for a sight of her. I went past the place I first saw her when she was nobody to me, when she was a good picture in a dark doorway. I stood there looking at the black space she'd filled. I missed her.

I only went back home because I imagined her sitting on Isabel's sofa, with Doormat on her lap, wondering what all the fuss was about.

She'd be pleased we were worrying about her. She'd say, "See? You didn't want me to go away at all, did you, Sam."

I wished so hard I hadn't said those things.

Isabel was angry with me at first when I told her. She said, "What did you say that to her for? Why are you taking your life out on a little girl?"

She said my trouble was I thought that people caring about me was a burden instead of a gift. "You want to be left alone," she said, "and Bo wants a mother like Doris Day. We can't always get what we want."

I stared at her table until my eyes blurred and I couldn't see it any more.

I never killed time like we did waiting for Bohemia to come home. You had to find fourteen thoughts just to fill one second, and one second lasted all day. Steve said it was just like flying, boredom and fear of the worst, combined.

Cherry came down and there was this stony silence when she walked in the room, from all of us. "I know, I know," she said. "You hate me. I get it."

She was shaking and she smoked cigarette after cigarette while we waited. The room filled with the low, thick fug of it. Without her make-up on you could see Bohemia in her face, in the flat of her cheekbones, in the delicate up-turn of her nose.

She looked at the clock a lot, at how little it had moved, and she rubbed at her eyes with the tips of her fingers. "Anyone got a drink?" she said.

Isabel stood up and put the kettle on. "You can have tea like the rest of us. Be sober for when she gets back."

Mick came in as well. He stood behind Cherry's chair and he put his hands on her shoulders.

Cherry didn't want to call the police either. That's maybe the one thing she and Isabel were ever going to agree on. She said, "I might never be ready to call those bastards."

"Those bastards might be the only hope you have of finding your daughter," Steve said.

"Look," Cherry said, "you hate me. Fair enough. I'm a crap mother."

"Yep," said Isabel.

"I'm a drunk and I like to party and I sleep around."

"You said it," Isabel folded her arms, ready for battle.

"She knows I love her," Cherry said frowning, picking at her nail varnish, pulling it off in pink flakes and scattering it on the table.

"No, she doesn't," I said. "She just knows she loves you."

I didn't mean to make Cherry cry. I was just saying what I thought. She put her head on the table and her hair spread out over the skin of her arms and she didn't make a scene or anything, her breath just kept catching and it made her nose run.

Nobody said anything. Isabel made her a cup of tea. Steve looked embarrassed, or slightly in pain or something. Mick stroked Cherry's hair. I put my arms on the table in front of her. I put my head down too.

"Sorry," I said.

Cherry looked over at me, her cheek resting on her arm. "Not as sorry as I am."

At some point in that first day I went to my room and found that Max's ant book with my money in it was gone. I searched around for it until I was sure it wasn't there.

I pictured Bohemia, swearing at me and hugging herself, hugging my book under her jumper. I was angry with her for maybe ten seconds. I stood by my bed and I balled up my fists and I roared, until Isabel banged on her ceiling and told me to give it a rest.

It was more than two hundred quid.

It scared me. It meant she wasn't coming back from the station this time. Not if she didn't want to. I went downstairs to tell the others.

"That's my girl," Cherry said, biting her fingernails.

"Bloody hell!" Isabel said.

What would you do with that much money if you were ten

and nobody was there to tell you? Live on sweets? Buy yourself a puppy? Give it to the nearest busker? I had this image of Bohemia stuffing my savings into the donations box at the National Gallery, walking away with a big Patron of the Arts smile on her face.

"She could be anywhere," I said.

Seventeen (Bohemia)

When I got off the coach at the right place, the ticket lady was watching me. I could feel her watching. I saw her head move when I moved, out of the corner of my eye. I held on to my coat really tight so none of the food fell out and I scratched my leg quickly to be sure of the money. In the car park I headed straight for the loo. I looked over my shoulder and said to my pretend family, "I need a wee." Them looking at me strangely was fine because it meant the lady on the coach stopped watching.

I stayed in the loo for a long time. There wasn't a lot to do in there and I had to take tiny breaths cos the dirty pine smell was quite overpowering. I washed my hands and face, but I couldn't see in the mirror cos it was too high so I just had to hope I looked tidy. The towel was on a roll and there wasn't one speck of it that hadn't been used at least forty times by someone else. I sorted out my pockets, food in one, Sam's book in the other, and I put all the crumbs and wrappers in the bin. The third time I peeked out into the grey and shiny metal of the car park, the coach had gone.

I was still quite a long way from where I needed to be.

There was a café on the corner and the smell of bacon was like this solid thing you could almost eat straight out of the air. Actually I had an egg because of the trying to be a vegetarian thing. I had a fried egg roll with ketchup and a glass of milk and a chocolate chip cookie as big as my face. Eggs are quite strange. I find them easier to eat if I don't look at them.

It took me *forever* to work out which bus I needed to get and what time it was coming and everything. I worked out that there was one bus in the morning and one in the afternoon, and I'd missed them.

That was it. One bus in the morning and one in the afternoon. Unbelievable.

I was standing there trying to think of what to do when a man got out of his car and asked me if I was OK. Everything he was wearing was the colour of a mushroom, even his shoes and bag and moustache.

I said, "I'm fine thanks," and I moved a little bit away from him sideways, not so he'd notice, not to be rude or anything, just to feel better.

"Are you lost?" he said.

"No."

"Where's your mum?"

What was I supposed to say to that? In bed with Mick. Passed out in the bathroom. Drunk in a corner.

I said, "She's gone to get some change for the meter."

He clucked his teeth and I looked at my shoes and I was starting to wonder if somebody who dresses like a mushroom could be described as dangerous. I was picturing myself running when a lady came out of the loo. I could tell straightaway she was his wife cos she looked like a mushroom too. Maybe that happens to you when you get old. You wake up and suddenly pale brown is your favourite colour.

I felt better that she was there. But then I remembered seeing this thing on TV once about a girl being followed by a big man. She got on a bus to get away from him and this nice old lady took pity on her and dried her tears and promised to take her home. Except the nice old lady was actually the big man's mum and she took the girl straight to him. I didn't sleep for days. It shows you can't be too careful.

"Her mum's gone for change," the man said to his wife.

"And left you here?" she said. "All by yourself?"

The whole of her throat, from her chin down to the top button of her shirt, swung and wobbled when she talked.

"I don't mind," I said, and I thought about how much her neck would wobble if she knew the half of it.

In the end I got a taxi. I felt bad about it being Sam's money, but I wasn't going to spend a whole night in the car park. It was cold for a start and it was probably going to rain, and I didn't want to sit and watch everything get empty and dark all by myself in a place I'd never been before. That's when it would've been handy to have Doormat, just for somebody to cuddle up to.

The people at the taxi place didn't believe me. I had to lie and lie to get them to take me.

I said my mum was a doctor and she was supposed to collect me from school, but she was stuck in the hospital.

I said my dad was away on business.

I said they couldn't speak to my mum cos she was busy in an emergency and that's why she couldn't take me herself.

They wanted to make sure I had the money. I felt a bit silly getting it out of my sock. It was crumpled and sweaty, but it changed their minds.

Forty quid it cost me. It was worth every penny.

Me and the driver didn't talk to each other. I put my face

against the window and I just stared and stared. Everything was so green. Everywhere was trees and fields, and the floor was all hills and slopes, not flat at all. And in the background, sort of brooding over all the green, was the purple and grey and brown and blue of the mountains. If it hadn't all been moving past at me at however many miles an hour, I'd have thought somebody drew a picture and stuck it to the window just to trick me.

We got stuck behind a tractor the size of a dinosaur, with red clods of mud dropping off its teeth, leaving red trails on the road behind it. The driver didn't like it. He kept trying to overtake, but the road was all windy and small and I didn't mind cos it gave me more time to look at things.

We got stuck in some sheep too, a whole load of them right there in the road. The farmer was waving his hands about, trying to get them to cross. It made a traffic jam. The sheep moved around the cars, both sides, behind and in front, and it was like we were in a boat and the bobbing sheep's backs were the foamy ripples of the sea.

We turned off the road and on to a track that was full of holes and ditches and puddles. It crunched under the tyres and the hedges either side of the car were too high to see over. The track was going up and up and up, and then suddenly the hedges disappeared and everything opened up and we were *right* at the bottom of the mountain, like a giant breathing down on us, standing really still. The track was just a tiny straight line in the middle of this wild place, thick with plants and dotted with sheep. They looked at the car and I looked back at them, and I remember thinking how lucky they were to live right there, and how I'd never in my whole life seen anything like it before.

After a bit the track bent round, and on the bend there was a house that looked like two houses stuck together. There were two dogs and three geese and a muddy car in the front. The taxi driver stopped and looked at me and said, "Home."

I paid him the money and I got my coat out of the back and I shut the door. Then I just stood there while he drove away cos I was suddenly feeling a bit nervous, like, what if no one was in or I had the wrong house or something?

I got Sam's book out of my pocket and I took small steps to the door. The dogs and the geese came to see me and smell my hands. The dogs wagged their tails and the geese shook their heads and feathers. I'd never been that close to a goose before. They're pretty big.

The front door was big too, and wooden and old. My hand hardly made any noise against it so I had to use the knocker, which was black and metal and loud.

A boy opened the door. He was tall like Sam, but much

thinner and his hair stuck out from his head in strange directions, like a paintbrush you forgot to wash. He had one blue sock on and one orange, and no shoes. He had a thing with his eyes, so that one was looking at me and one was looking at something behind me, just above my head. He had two thin, jagged scars, one above his right eye that disappeared into his hair, and one under his lip, all across his chin. He had some teeth missing too, gaps like mine except he was way too old for that.

He was leaning on a stick, leaning heavily, like if you took it away from him he might just collapse in a heap, right there. He didn't smile, he frowned, and his mouth was open, but he didn't say anything.

He wasn't quite what I expected.

"Are you Max?" I said, and he nodded.

"Max the Ant Expert?"

He shifted his stick and thought about it, and then he nodded again.

"Thank God for that," I said. "I'm Bohemia. I'm a friend of Sam's. I've brought you your book back."

Eighteen (Sam)

It was impossible to even try to sleep the first night Bohemia was away. We sat round Isabel's table like waxworks, not talking, hardly moving, just suspended in time. Cherry ran out of cigarettes and started drumming softly on the tabletop with the tips of her fingers. Mick watched her constantly, like he expected her to fall apart any minute. Steve couldn't take his eyes off the clock. Isabel heated up some soup and we all ate without really tasting it.

I was supposed to be at work, but there's no way I was going.

Isabel said I had to go and tell them. She said I'd lose my job if I didn't.

"I don't care," I said.

"Course you do. Think about it."

I thought about not working and not having any money

to pay the rent and having to leave and go home. I thought about not being here when Bohemia came back.

"I'll go and tell them," I said.

Cherry said she was coming with me. She said, "I need some fags and I could do with the air."

Mick asked if she wanted him to go with her. She said he didn't need to. She said, "I could do with being on my own."

As if me being there didn't count.

It was cold outside and Cherry rubbed the tops of her arms through her T-shirt. "I should've got my jacket," she said.

I gave her my sweatshirt to put on. I took it off and handed it to her, the same one I'd given to Bohemia in the park.

"Oh, it's warm," she said, pulling it over her head, slipping both arms in at once.

It's exactly what Bohemia had said.

Cherry didn't come in the shop. She gave me the money for her cigarettes and stood outside in the cold, her hands in her pockets, looking up at the sky. I told Besnik's uncle that something had come up. I said there was an emergency and I couldn't work tonight. He shrugged and looked at the far corner of his shop while he was talking.

He said, "There are hundreds of boys just like you wanting jobs."

I said, "I want my job. I just need tonight off. Maybe tomorrow. Hopefully not."

"Two shifts," he said. "After two shifts it's somebody else's."

Outside, Cherry unwrapped the packet and dropped the rubbish on the floor. I had to hold my hands around the flame of her lighter because the wind kept blowing it out. We walked slower on the way back. I think maybe we were giving Bohemia more time to get there first.

When we got to the park at the end of the road she wanted to sit there for a bit. She asked me if I'd sit with her. She said, "I don't want to go back in there and carry on waiting."

The park was empty except for a couple lying on a blanket by the bins. They looked like they were sunbathing in the dark. We sat on the third bench in from the entrance. Cherry lit a new cigarette with the end of the last one.

"I haven't had a drink today," she said.

I didn't answer. I just listened because I had the feeling that's what she wanted me to do.

"I can't tell you the last time I didn't have a drink."

She looked at her cigarette then and she threw it on the floor away from her, half smoked. She twisted her hair around with her right hand and tucked it in at her collar. She looked almost as lost in my sweatshirt as Bohemia had.

She said, "I'm praying to God she's all right. I'm praying and I don't even believe in God."

She said, "I don't know where she could've gone. There isn't anyone for her to go to."

She said, "She's only got me."

And then she folded forwards with her elbows on her knees and said very quietly to the floor, "I'm a terrible mother. I'm a bad, bad person."

"No you're not," I said, because I had to, but we both knew that neither of us believed it.

She said, "I was so young when I had her. I was your age."

She said, "Maybe we should be calling the police right now."

She said, "If she comes home in one piece, I'll never drink or smoke or do drugs or leave her behind again."

It was quiet then while we both listened to the echoes in our heads of what she'd just said.

"Do you think you could do that?" I asked her.

She shrugged and started chewing at her nails. "I'd like to," she said. Then she sat up straight again and looked at me. "What's the worst thing you've ever done?" she said.

I said she didn't want to know.

"Yes, I do," she said. "I bet it's nothing. What is it? Stealing sweets from the newsagents? Looking at porn mags in your dad's shed?"

"It's not nothing," I said.

"Well, I bet it is compared to me. I threw my own child away, Sam. What did you do? Come on, take my mind off it, I could do with a laugh."

And so I told her, partly to prove her wrong, and partly because it's easy telling someone how low you've sunk when they're further down than you.

Nineteen (Bohemia)

Being with Max was *very* confusing. When I gave him the book, he looked at it for a long time and then he said, "OK," instead of "Thanks," and he started shutting the door with me still on the outside of it.

"Can I come in?" I said, and the door stopped closing.

He frowned at me.

I said, "I've come quite a long way."

He didn't say anything. He just opened the door enough for me to walk through and then he followed me down the corridor into the kitchen. His stick thwacked on the hard floor and his foot dragged.

The kitchen was about the size of our whole flat, by the way. And there was a big wooden table in there that you could fit everyone in our whole house around.

Max went to the sink and poured me a glass of water. He pushed a bowl of fruit in my direction and I took a banana and a handful of grapes out of it.

"Why have you got my book?" he said.

It was on the table between us. *The Ant Colony* by Dr Bernard O Hopkins.

"I stole it from Sam," I said. "I stole all his money as well, but not on purpose, and then I borrowed some to come and give this to you."

I opened the front cover and turned it towards him. "See?" I said. "Your name and address. That's how come I knew where to find you."

"OK," he said.

"I tried to read some on the coach," I said, "but it was *way* too hard for me."

Max's eyes were very dark blue. He had long eyelashes like a girl.

I said, "Sam told me you were clever." He blinked. I said, "Don't you want to know where he is?"

He laughed then, sort of, and shook his head, and looked at me like I was a funny thing that just fell out of his sock. "Sam?" he said again.

"He should've left a note," I said. "I told him that. You've got every right to be cross with him."

I said, "I'm sure he would've sent a note with me, except he didn't know I was coming."

I said, "It's kind of a surprise."

I wanted Max to say something. I wanted him to be pleased that Sam was somewhere and not disappeared off the face of the earth. It wasn't turning out like I imagined at all.

"Sam told me all about you, Max," I said.

He frowned, picked up the book and opened it just anywhere and started reading. It was rude, I thought, just to start reading like that while I was talking to him. "Is it really a good book?" I said.

"It's a brilliant book," he said. "Sam didn't read it."

"Well, he took it all the way to London with him," I said. "And he didn't take much. You should see his flat. It's *empty*. Why would he take it if he wasn't going to read it?"

"So he's in London," Max said.

Then this woman's voice just outside the door said, "Who's in London?" and when she came in the room and saw me she said, "Who's this?"

"Sam's in London," Max said. "This girl brought my book back."

The woman stopped dead still in the middle of the kitchen and she stared at me. "Oh, God," she said.

Max picked up the book, like he was sort of hiding behind it.

She said it again. "Oh, God."

I looked at her and I looked at the book in front of Max's face, and I said, "It's OK. He's really fine."

"Who *are* you?" she said.

"I'm Bo," I said. "I'm Sam's friend."

"Well, I am not," she told me, and I could see she meant it *really* hard cos her hands were in fists and her knuckles were like bone white from squeezing.

"Not what?" I said.

"Sam's *friend*," she said. "And nor is my son."

I didn't get it *at* all.

"What do you mean?" I said. "Is that true?"

Max said, "Yes, but it's good to see my book."

Twenty (Sam)

The worst thing I did when I was eleven was tell some of the kids at my new school that Max was a weirdo and he liked pickling ants. It got me a laugh, but it didn't do him any favours at all. It kind of cemented his reputation.

The worst thing I did when I was eleven and still Max's best friend was realise that he was never going to make me popular. That everyone saw Max for the ways he was different, and that the ways he was different were rubbing off on me.

The worst thing I did when I was eleven was switch sides and laugh at him along with everybody else, and leave him in the playground on his own, a wounded frown on his face, one eye looking at the tree tops, one eye looking straight at me.

The worst thing I did when I was eleven was pretend to be his friend for long enough to copy his homework or borrow his calculator or get him to lend me money.

The worst thing I did while I was at school was want people not to like Max, because I wanted the person they hated not to be me.

He was an easy target. If you laughed at him he just blinked at you slowly, because he never quite understood why things were funny. If you flicked him on the back of the head when you walked past him in the corridor, he always said "Ouch" to the floor. If you saw him in the woods while you were all at the river, dressed in his ant-hunting gear, with a flask of water and a compass and a specimen jar and a clipboard, and you chased him and threw his things into the water, he waded in, fully clothed, and got them out and didn't look you in the eye, not once.

The first night I climbed up the side of his house to his window, I took pictures of him asleep with his eye patch on, and we stuck them up around the school for people to see. That was the worst thing I did when I was fourteen. The headteacher prowled up and down the assembly hall waiting for the culprit to own up. I never did.

His mum and dad came to see mine. They said, "This victimisation has to *stop*."

I denied everything. I said it was nothing to do with me. I said I'd tried to have a word on Max's behalf, but when a whole school was against somebody it was difficult for one person to make them stop.

Max's mum looked at me like she hated me that night, like I was the most despicable person she'd ever met.

I don't blame her.

Max didn't act like he hated me. That's the other thing that made picking on him so easy. Whatever I did, or helped others to do, the next day he'd nod and say, "Hello, Sam," like we were still friends, like nothing bad had ever happened to him because of me. It was as if, in spite of everything, Max liked me, for old times' sake. It made me think I had nothing to feel bad about. It made it easier for me to kid myself, put it that way.

The worst thing I did when I was seventeen was the worst thing I've ever done. Worse even than disappearing without leaving a note, worse even than making Bohemia do the same.

It was October and my dad was giving me driving lessons up on the common – boring, meticulous, mirror-signal-manoeuvre lessons, when all I wanted to do was let rip and do handbrake turns and look at myself in the rearview mirror with my good shades on. I was desperate to learn to drive. Living in the middle of nowhere can do that to a person. I was sick of getting lifts all the time and cycling up hills until I felt like my lungs were going to bleed. I hassled the life out of my dad to start teaching me. I talked about nothing but driving until he gave in.

I remember sitting in the car with him every Thursday at five, watching the reined-in, concrete profile of his face, the way he set his jaw when I did something wrong and the car squealed.

Once I remember saying, "Can I have a car for my birthday then or what?"

He laughed. He said the best I could hope for was to pick one up at the dump and get my genius friend Max to fix it up.

"Max?" I said. "What are you on about?"

He said, "His dad was telling me all about it last night in the pub. Max read a few books about mechanics, got a car from the scrap yard and he's putting the thing back together. He's got it in a shed up at the house. It bloody works too."

"That's interesting," I said.

"I know," Dad looked at me. "Is there nothing that boy can't do?"

I started being nicer to Max then. Not in public or anything, not so anyone would notice. I think Max noticed though. It was around then that Mum dropped him at his house after chess club, or that I walked the dog near his house so I could have an excuse to bump into him. I wanted to see the car.

I wish I'd never set eyes on it now.

I was walking Ringo on the common. It was starting to get dark. He started barking at something I couldn't see in the half-light. He ran off with his hackles up, storming across the bracken towards whatever was there. I followed him. I could hear the shush and thump of him running. I could see less and less with every few paces, like the light was just falling out of a hole in the sky.

It was Max and his car. He was just sitting in it with the engine and the lights off. He was waiting for me to leave.

"Shit, Max," I said, circling it, keeping my hand on it all the way round. I was acting like I owned it already. I can see that when I watch myself from here.

Max nodded. He wound down his window. "Hello, Sam."

"Nice car," I said.

He was sitting very still and looking straight ahead, like I hadn't seen him yet, like he was still pretending he wasn't there.

I put my elbows on his open window and leaned in. "Give us a go," I said.

He smiled. He shook his head.

"I can drive," I said. "My dad's been teaching me."

"No, Sam," he said.

I stood up again, looked around me, breathed out. There was no way I could be this close to it and not drive it. "Let me drive to the cattle grid," I said. "Ringo can follow us. And then I'll get out and walk him home down the road."

"Why should I?" he said, very quietly. I got the feeling that if I hadn't heard it the first time, he wouldn't have said it again.

"Oh, mate," I said. "You're the first person in our year to have a car. You're the coolest. You're going to have no worries now."

Max looked at me then. He said, "Do you promise?"

I smiled and opened the door for him to get out. "I wouldn't lie to you about that," I said, and I was in the driver's seat before he'd walked round the car and opened the door at the other side.

I started off pretty slowly. I acted like my dad was in the car with me. I put my seatbelt on. I checked my mirrors. I put the lights on full beam and they sliced out across the common, bleaching the night out of the bracken, marking out the last dancing of the flies. Ringo was barking and wagging his tail behind us. I could just see him in the lights. We bumped sedately along towards the cattle grid.

"I'll get out just up here," I said.

But I didn't.

Just before the grid I swung the car to the right and put my foot down hard.

"Stop!" Max shouted at me. "What are you doing?"

"Just one more lap."

Ringo's bark was further away now and the bracken crumpled fast in the lights. I remember seeing the moon quite low in the sky ahead of us. I remember having time to notice there were stars. I remember Max was shouting, but I didn't listen.

Three times we went round, three great loops of the common in the dark. The last time was fast. I looked at Max. He was quiet now and he was crying.

I laughed at him. I said, "What's the matter?"

He didn't answer me. He wiped his nose with the back of his hand.

I said, "What's the point of owning your own car if you're not going to really *drive* it?"

Remembering that moment is hard. Seeing myself behind the wheel, grinning and yelling, it's like looking at someone I hate. It's like looking at someone I made disappear.

Because just after that Max shouted something. And at the same time we hit it. Two things. We hit something that sent us hurtling into a rock. There was a deep sudden thud and the force of it turned forty miles an hour into nothing in a second. I felt the speed we'd been going rush past us from behind, slamming my face towards the steering wheel, knocking the air out of my lungs, throwing me against my own seatbelt so hard that I had bruises across my chest for weeks.

Max wasn't wearing his.

He hit the windscreen. He smashed through it with his face. He somersaulted over the front of the bonnet and hit the ground, surrounded by falling glass that blinked like diamonds in the headlights' glare.

It happened so fast, but I always remember it in slow motion. In my memory it is crammed with little details.

My hands were shaking so much I couldn't open the door. I climbed out of the hole Max had made. There was glass and blood all over my clothes.

"Max?" I said. "Are you all right, mate?"

He was quiet. He was curled up in a ball on the ground.

That's one of the things I remember, how quiet it was after all that noise, how the slam and judder and smash had left a hole in the noise behind them after they were gone.

I could hear the engine still running and the oblivious call of a night bird.

I remember thinking, *None of this is really happening. Somewhere in the real world I'm getting out of Max's car at the cattle grid and walking Ringo home, just like I said I would.*

I couldn't get him to hear me.

I was shouting then, "HELP!" and all kinds of stuff, and there was nobody around.

Then I remembered my phone and I crouched by the headlights to try and see what I was dialling. I couldn't understand how to make my own phone work.

The front of the car was caved in and dark with blood.

I couldn't get any signal.

I had to walk to Max's house across the common. I had to leave him there, curled up in the black. I ran most of the way and then I couldn't run any more.

It wasn't until I got there that I realised I was bleeding. Max's mum opened the door and she put her hands over her eyes, just for a second. Then she took my hand and I saw it was wet with blood, blood dripping from the ends of my fingers like rich paint. I'd cut my wrist on the windscreen climbing out. There was a piece of glass in there, sticking out, one of Max's diamonds. It wasn't so bad.

Max's dad said I was lucky it wasn't an artery. He called an ambulance.

"What happened to you?" Max's mum said. She had her

arm around me and was taking me to a chair. She'd never been that nice to me before. I was thinking that and I knew I was about to put an end to it forever.

"The ambulance has to go to the common," I said.

"What for?"

"He's still up there," I said. "We have to go. He's not saying anything."

That's when she went white, in an instant. Her face changed shape entirely and she said, "Oh no. No."

"What have you done?" she said.

Max's dad drove. We could see the lights of Max's car and we bumped and rattled along towards the dome of lesser dark they were making.

"What have you done to him?" she asked me.

I didn't say anything. I didn't feel like all of me was there.

"I told you," she said to Max's dad. "I *told* you he was dangerous. I said this would happen."

"Is that enough now?" she turned and shouted at me in the car. "Have you finished?" I could see the curve of her eyes glinting in the dark.

Max's dad didn't say anything. He didn't need to.

I thought about what I must look like to them, this boy sitting in the back of their car with a tea towel round his arm; this boy responsible for so much pain.

Max was still curled up. I remember his mum making noises like a wild animal. I remember her touching him so timidly, like she was afraid of what she might find.

He rolled open under her hand, limp and boneless. His face was a mask of blood.

I thought he was dead.

We all did.

In the morning, while I was still at the hospital, my mum and dad went up to the common to see for themselves what had happened. The car was there, cratered and folded up all alone in the early mist. The engine and the lights were off. I don't know if anyone did that – Max's dad or the ambulance driver – or if they just ran out on their own, hours later, with nobody watching. There was a patch of flat bracken where Max had landed. His blood had soaked into the earth. If they'd looked hard enough they'd have found three of his teeth.

What they found instead was Ringo, spread out on his side, tyre tracks either side of him. Some way behind the car, cold and open-eyed and lifeless, his dry tongue flung out against the wet ground.

They said the impact of the car didn't leave a mark on him.

Twenty-one (Bohemia)

I had it coming I suppose, cos I asked Max about his scars. I couldn't help myself. They were the things I couldn't stop looking at on his face. "What happened to you?" I said, and I pointed to my eye and chin so he'd know what I was asking.

"Accident," he said.

"No it wasn't," his mum said.

"Yes it was."

"Ouch," I said.

He smiled at me for the first time when I said that. He said, "It doesn't hurt any more."

"What sort of accident?" I said.

"Sam Cassidy," his mum said from where she was standing at the sink, cutting apples into quarters, peeling them in one long twirl.

"Don't, Mum," he said.

"What do you mean, *Sam Cassidy*?" I said.

"I mean the accident of ever knowing him," she said with her back to me. "I mean the accident of living near him, of ever being nice to him, of *him*, full stop."

Boy, she was an angry one. You could tell just by the way she was treating those apples. "I don't get it," I said.

So she told me. About Sam stealing Max's car with him in it. About crashing in the dark. About Max being in hospital for ages and never being the same again. About Ringo being dead and everything.

Max said, "Mum, you don't have to," and "I don't think she wants to hear this," but once she started talking she wasn't going to stop.

She said, "He broke your *neck*, Max. You're lucky to be alive. You're lucky you can walk."

She said, "Max lost three pints of blood. *Three pints*."

She said, "The only decent thing Sam Cassidy ever did was disappear." She pointed her knife at me while she was talking. "That boy nearly killed my son. He spent years tormenting him and then he nearly *killed* him."

It would have been better if I'd known before. I would have preferred it if Sam hadn't lied to me, cos I felt a bit of a fool sitting there at his best friend's biggest-kitchen-table-ever, finding out how much his best friend hated him.

"He didn't mean to," I said afterwards. "He wouldn't have meant to."

"Ha!" Max's mum said, and her voice alone could have skinned the apples. "I suppose he didn't mean to do all the other things either. He didn't mean to throw Max's camera in the river, or humiliate him at school, or tell lies about him, or make sure he never got one good friend."

I said, "I'm sorry. But your Sam isn't the same as mine."

"What do you mean?" she said.

I said that my Sam would *never* be mean or pick on someone or take their stuff and not look after it. She looked at me like I'd be funny if I wasn't so stupid.

I said, "My Sam rescued me when I was locked out in the dark and he looks after me, and he walks Isabel's dog and fixes her cupboards, and he took me to the National Gallery just so I'd like my hair, and he stopped me from being a shoplifter and he wants to help my mum and..." I looked at Max. "He talks about you a lot," I said. "I thought you were *best friends*."

"Why would he say that?" Max said.

"I don't know," I said. "He doesn't talk much, cos he can't get a word in edgeways, but when he does, he talks about you."

"Guilt," Max's mum said. "Shame."

"And he *loves* his dog," I said. "He told me all about Ringo. He said he was big enough for me to ride."

"He was massive," Max said, and the way he said it was all lispy cos of the gaps in his teeth.

It made me so sad to think about Sam, and nobody knowing where he was, and him pretending that his dead dog and this boy that he hurt were the things he loved best in the world.

I just couldn't understand it at all.

I said, "Well, I don't know what to do now. I came all this way by myself cos I thought you would help me."

Max said, "Help you do what?"

And his mum said, "What do you mean, all by yourself?"

So first I told her about walking to the coach station in the middle of the night. I told her about blending in with other people's families and being really good at thinking up a lie on the spot when you have to, and about being invisible, and how it's actually quite easy if you think about it hard enough.

She said, "Doesn't anybody know you're here? Your mum or your dad?"

I said my dad would be pretty surprised to find out where I was cos he last saw me when I was a tiny baby.

"Well, your mum then."

"She won't mind too much," I said. "She's probably out."

"So she knows?"

"No, but it's OK. I'll be back by tomorrow."

Max's mum didn't get it. She said, "That doesn't make sense."

I told her that was cos she wasn't my mum.

"Well, we have to phone her," she said. "What's her number?"

"It's not working. She didn't pay her bill."

She said, "There must be somebody we can call."

I said that's what I wanted help with.

"Can we call Sam's mum and dad?" I said. "I want to tell them he's OK."

She didn't want to do that, you could just tell by the way her shoulders went up and she stopped chopping apples.

But Max said, "Good idea," and dialled the number. He passed me the phone while it was still ringing.

The room went very quiet apart from that ringing in my ear, and then a voice said, "Hello?" It was a woman's voice, and she was quiet and trembly and sad.

"Is that Sam's mum?" I said, and she said it was and who was I?

"My name's Bo," I said. "Bohemia Hoban. I'm a friend of Sam's."

There wasn't any noise at the other end, it was just nothing, and I thought the phone might've gone dead.

"Hello?" I said.

"He's not here," she said.

"I know."

"Then why did you call?"

I looked at Max's mum's back then, at the way she'd stopped moving, and at Max's dark blue eyes. I said, "I called cos I wanted to tell you where he is."

Twenty-two (Sam)

Cherry didn't laugh when I finished telling her. She watched me drag my stupid, nasty, unforgivable self into my brand new life. She listened. And when I went quiet she said, "Shit, Sam, that's unbelievable."

"I know," I said.

She asked me what happened next.

"Max was in a coma for three days," I said.

"But he didn't die though."

"No. He woke up. I was waiting in the corridor, but they wouldn't let me see him."

"Not surprised," Cherry said.

"Me neither. He broke his neck."

An ambulance went past on the road, lights and sirens on. It shattered the quiet of the park.

"Is he paralysed?' she said.

"I don't know," I said. "I heard he was learning to walk with a stick. I heard all the damage was on one side of his body."

"Poor Max," she said.

That's what my mum said when she found out the truth about everything. She was so relieved her son hadn't been hurt, and so disgusted at the person her son had turned out to be.

"Poor Max," she said, sometimes out loud and sometimes without even having to speak. "I can't believe we didn't listen to him. I'm so ashamed you did this."

My dad didn't speak at all. I think he kept out of my way. I don't think he wanted to look at me.

We buried Ringo. I couldn't stop crying and they just glared at me over the grave from the other side, the mound of newly dug earth between us, their eyes like stones.

I think they hated me. For taking their love all these years and not being who they thought I was. I'm sure they hated me.

"What happened then?" Cherry asked.

"Well, everyone knew straightaway. News like that travels fast in a small town."

"What did they say?"

"Not much, not to me. Everyone kept away. It was something

to talk about. It was something beginning with, 'Oh my GOD, have you heard?'"

"What about your friends?"

"You know what? That's the worst bit. Some of them thought it was *funny*. They said they'd miss the dog more than they'd miss Max and that he didn't deserve a car anyway, stuff like that."

I remember listening to them and thinking, *Are these the people I've been trying to impress? Am I like them?*

Truth was, I was worse.

"Did you see Max again?" she asked me.

"Yes. Once."

"What happened?"

"I said sorry."

"What did he say?"

"He said, *I don't forgive you.*"

"I bet he did. You can't blame him. And then?"

"And then I disappeared."

"No you didn't."

"Yes I did."

"I can see you," she said.

"OK, I came here."

"Because you thought your mum and dad were never going to forgive you, and Max was never going to forgive you?"

"Yep."

"Because you couldn't live with yourself any more, right?"

"Something like that."

"Jesus, Sam, what a mess."

I looked at the path between my feet, at the dead leaves and litter under the bench. I laughed, sort of quietly. "Yeah, because guess who was here when I arrived?"

She shrugged. "Me and Mick and Steve and Isabel and Bohemia."

"And Doormat."

"God, OK, and Doormat."

"And me. *I* was here."

"Oh, I get it."

"I can't run away," I said. "I'm still responsible. It's still my fault, wherever I am."

Cherry sighed and looked away from me at some random point in the sky. "When did you work that out?" she said.

"Don't know. Just now."

She said, "The only way not to live with yourself is to get so out of it you can't remember your own name. Even that doesn't last very long. Trust me, I know."

"Yeah, well, I'm going to give your method a miss if you don't mind."

Cherry looked at me and smiled, and I could see she was

thinking about Bohemia at the same time because it was the saddest smile I'd ever seen.

"You're a clever kid," she said. "And I don't mind at all. I'm thinking of doing the same thing myself. If she comes back, I'll change, that's a promise."

It was quiet for a minute and then she said, "Where the hell do you think she's gone?"

I said I didn't know.

She said, "I've done a runner so many times. I never thought about how it would feel to be the one left behind." She lit a cigarette and blew smoke and warm breath out into the cold air. "Is it anything like you imagined?"

I said I tried not to imagine it.

"I suppose when you run away and pretend to disappear," she said, "you pretend that everything you left behind disappears too. But it doesn't."

We looked at each other. Cherry was right. Bohemia was gone and nothing else had disappeared. It was all still there. We were still there, waiting on a park bench. The others were still trapped in Isabel's kitchen, all of us watching the stopped clocks until Bohemia walked through the door and made them start again.

I realised that what Isabel had been trying to tell me about running, Bohemia had shown me first hand. And that maybe the more we sat there and thought about it, the more Cherry and I saw that our new lives were exactly the same as our old ones, because we were still in them.

"Come on," she said, getting up. "I can't sit here any more. We've got to do something."

Everyone was in the same place when we got back, in exactly the same position. Mick tried to give Cherry a hug, but she kind of slipped out of it, under his arm, and she said, "I can't do that right now. Don't comfort me, for God's sake,"

He said, "Sorry."

Cherry looked at Isabel and she said, "What are we going to say to them? To the police?"

"I don't know," Isabel said.

The room felt wretched and airless.

Steve said, "The first thing they'll do is search the park, and the wasteland between us and the canal, and other people's houses."

"Wasteland?" Cherry said.

Isabel scowled at him. "That's a bit harsh," she said. "You don't pull any punches, do you."

"OK, maybe someone will remember selling her a ticket somewhere," Steve said, "and then we can find out where she's gone."

I couldn't look at Cherry suddenly. It was like she couldn't hold herself together much longer. She was making these little noises while she breathed and she had her hands over her mouth like she was trying to push the sounds back in.

"Do you want us to phone them?" Isabel said.

"I want her back," Cherry said, and her voice was different.

"I know, dear," said Isabel, and she squeezed Cherry's hand across the table.

Cherry said, "I want her back so I can look after her."

"Yes."

Cherry looked at Mick and her eyes were so scared, so hollow with it, she looked like a different person. "I didn't look after her," she said.

Mick looked at Isabel and then at Cherry. Isabel didn't let go of her hand. "You did your best, baby," he said.

Cherry was shaking her head. "No," she said. "No, I didn't."

When the phone rang it cut through us all like a scream. Isabel made a lunge for it.

"Who the hell's that?" she said before she picked it up, and then, "Hello? Hello?"

I was thinking it was the police and whether that was good news or bad. I was thinking it might be a wrong number, or a consumer survey, or one of those recordings that tells you you've won a new kitchen. I was thinking that I hadn't heard Isabel's phone ring once in all the time that I'd been there. I didn't even know she had one.

And then she said, "Sam? Yes, he's here," and she passed it to me.

I watched the old spiral of cord stretch and open as she passed it.

I said, "Who could be calling me here?"

Isabel put the receiver in my hand and moved my hand to my ear.

"It's your mum," she said.

"Hello?" My mum was saying. "Hello, darling, is that you?" And then she was crying and I was crying too, and everyone in Isabel's kitchen was watching me.

I said, "I'm sorry, Mum," and she said, "Come home and say that."

I said, "I'm different now," and she said, "I want to see you."

I asked her how she found me.

"A little girl came today, to the house. She came with Max. Bohemia."

"Bohemia?" I said.

Twenty-three (Sam)

We all went up in Steve's car. It was an old Cortina and none of us thought it was going to make it, except for Steve.

He suggested it as soon as Cherry put the phone down. Suddenly the clocks were ticking and the room was full of air again. She said, "She's OK, she's fine," and she was crying, but she looked like herself again.

"She's with your mum?" Mick said to me.

"Yeah. She's at my house."

"How did she get all that way on her own?" said Isabel. "How did she know where to go?"

"We'll ask her when we get there," Steve said. "What are we waiting for? Let's go!"

"What, all of us?" I said.

They all stopped what they were doing then, Isabel putting the phone back on the table, Mick clearing the cups, Steve putting on his jacket, Cherry with her hands in her hair. They stopped and looked at me like they were one being, not four.

"Of course *all of us*," Isabel said. "Who were you thinking of leaving behind?"

Isabel sat in the front with the dog between her feet. Whenever Steve took a corner she did this sharp intake of breath and said, "It's OK, Doormat, calm down," like Doormat was the one that was worried.

I sat in the back with Cherry and Mick. He had his arm round her and she put her head on his shoulder and smiled at me. "I can't believe it," she said. "She's safe. She made it all the way to your mum's."

We stopped at a service station halfway there because none of us had eaten all day and good news had suddenly made us starving, and according to Isabel, Doormat needed to pee and stretch his legs. It was over-bright in there after the motion of the road. Isabel and Cherry had to go to the ladies' and Steve needed a coffee and Mick said he could do with a fry up. I got a sandwich and sat on a green plastic bench waiting for them all to come back.

One old and deeply wrinkled lady in an overcoat and flip flops.

One blonde woman, hair scraped back, biting her nails, still wearing my sweatshirt.

One lizard in shades and a leather jacket.

One man with a gun tattooed on his leg and a ridiculous beard.

I watched them, each one, and I thought how odd they looked alone, how I wouldn't have picked one of them out in a line-up of my future friends, not in a million years.

"What are you smiling at?" Isabel said.

"Nothing," I said, because I couldn't tell them how good it felt to be part of something so unexpected. I wouldn't know where to start.

I went to London to be on my own and I ended up being the opposite. Maybe it was like Dr Bernard O Hopkins said in the only page of *The Ant Colony* I'd ever bothered to read – that ants on their own can't accomplish much of anything, but together they can do the unthinkable.

After the motorway ended, the roads were unlit and wound over the mountain in hair-pins and arcs. Steve drove slowly. The headlights picked out the hedgerows either side of us, the bends ahead.

"Oh my God," Mick said with his head out of the back window. "Look at all those stars."

"What a place to grow up," Steve said.

Cherry put her hand on my arm. "Are you all right?" she said.

"Course I am. About what?"

"About seeing your mum and dad and stuff."

"I don't know," I said. "I think so."

"It'll be fine," she said.

I thought about it, about seeing them again. About seeing Max and his mum and dad. About coming back different. About convincing them all that I wasn't the same.

I thought about Bohemia coming all this way, acting like the magnet to pull us all together and pull us all here.

The Story of My Life
Part Five
by B Hoban

When Mum said we were moving into Mick's flat I wasn't sure about it. I said I didn't see why we had to.

Mum said, "It's bigger."

I said, "He doesn't really want me there."

She said, "Are you kidding? Wait till you see what he's done for you."

"What's he done?" I said.

"I can't tell you," she said. "He'll be cross if I ruin the surprise."

"Well, when can I see?"

"Maybe later. It's nearly finished."

I'll tell you what it was. A room. An actual room of my own. Mick had painted it pink and the floor was white and the bed was pink and white too. There was a desk and a chest of drawers and everything. All painted to match. Our star lampshade was hanging from the ceiling. It was like a room from a magazine. It was like the most beautiful room I ever saw.

Mum and Mick just stood there in the doorway with their arms round each other, grinning at me.

I didn't know where to look first. Inside the desk was all pens and paper, and inside the chest of drawers was new clothes folded up and tidy.

"The clothes are from Steve," Mick said.

Mum said, "And the pens are from Isabel, for when you start school."

We went round the house and we told everybody, even though they knew already, and it turned into a party down at Isabel's.

I phoned Sam. I said, "I got my own room."

"No way," he said. "Wait till I tell Max."

"I know," I said. "Isn't that the best news ever?"

Twenty-four (Bohemia)

I remember waking up at Sam's mum's house, before it was properly light. I looked out of the window and there was this thick white fog, all around us. The sound of the wind in the trees sounded like the sea and I thought, *I wasn't by the sea when I went to sleep.*

I was in Sam's room. After his mum kissed me goodnight and shut the door, I got out of bed and had a good look around at his stuff. It was nice to see it all there, books and posters and CDs and a computer and football boots and pens and pencils and a globe that lit up when you plugged it in and clothes everywhere.

I thought he must have felt so far from home in his empty room in London.

When Max came with me to Sam's house, Sam's mum

and dad were really surprised to see him. Max's mum drove us over, but she wouldn't come in and she wouldn't stay. "Just give me a ring," she said, "when you want me to come and get you."

It took Max quite a long time to get out of the car cos his right leg needed some encouragement. His mum opened her door to go round and help, but he told her not to. He said, "I'm fine, Mum. I can do it myself."

She watched him in her mirror, and I turned away and looked at where Sam lived, cos I wanted to see it and cos I didn't think Max needed an audience.

Sam's house was low and made of golden stone and the windows were all blue. And right behind the house, towering up and over it was a mountain. I could see trees leaning over in the wind near the top, and sheep like little white dots.

Sam's mum and dad opened the door before we got there.

"Max," they said, and they were looking at him like they were searching his eyes for something.

"You look well," Sam's dad said, and Max smiled and said, "Thanks, Mr Cassidy. I'm feeling much better."

Sam's mum had tears in her eyes already and she was smiling through them at Max, and then she looked at me. "Hello," she said. "Are you Bohemia?"

I said I was.

"And you're Sam's friend?"

"Yes," I said. "And I'm Max's now too."

They smiled at me and then they both looked back at Max. "She's very young," Sam's dad said, and then to me, "How old are you, Bohemia?"

"I'm ten," I said. "I'm older than I look."

Sam's mum said, "Well, this is all such a surprise. Come in."

Max was concentrating quite hard on getting his foot up over the step. Everybody was waiting.

"That's it, Max," I said. "You've nearly done it."

We sat in a room with soft chairs that looked out at the mountain. Sam's mum offered us a drink, but you could see she just wanted to find out about Sam.

"Let's talk first," Max said.

She sat down then, on the arm of her husband's chair. They held hands. They were much older than Cherry, but you could still see which bits of them made Sam. His dad's long legs and big feet and eyebrows, his mum's hair and nose and mouth. I was smiling at them so hard. I couldn't help it.

"It's good," Max said. "What Bohemia has to tell you is good."

They both looked at me then and you could see they were holding their breath, so I told them.

There was a picture of Sam on a shelf above the fire. I said,

"That's Sam, right?" and I pointed at it and they nodded.

I said, "Sam lives at 33 Georgiana Street, Camden Town, London, and I think he misses you and he'd like to come home."

Sam's mum's mouth opened and it wouldn't close again. She was smiling with her mouth open and she tried to stand up, but Sam's dad had hold of her hand and he said, "Wait a minute now, Suzie, wait a minute."

He said, "How do you know this, Bohemia?"

"Cos I live there too," I said. "With my mum Cherry, and Mick I suppose, at the moment."

"And why are you here?"

"Oh, cos me and Sam had a fight and I stole Max's address."

"I see."

"I wanted to make him not cross with me. I wanted him to stop being ALONE all the time. He's always going on about being ALONE and he doesn't even like it."

Sam's mum was crying quietly.

I said, "I'm sorry about your dog. I didn't know about any of that till I got here."

She said, "Does 33 Georgiana Street have a phone number? Do you think we could speak to our son?"

It took me a minute to remember Isabel's number. I said, "It's either a three at the end or a seven."

Sam's mum tried the three first. It was the seven.

I can't remember what she said when Isabel answered, but I knew she heard Sam's voice cos she just cried and cried, and she was smiling her heart out at the same time.

When she told Sam that I was there, I sort of sank back in my chair a bit cos I did steal from him and stuff, and last time I saw him he was pretty angry. But when she said my name again, "Yes, Bohemia," she held the phone away from her ear and I could hear them, all of them at home, cheering and calling my name. I could hear Cherry the loudest.

I didn't know who to smile at.

Sam's mum was looking at me then and listening to Sam, and her eyes were getting bigger and bigger. I thought maybe he was telling her about the money and I was going to get in trouble.

Then she said, "Bohemia, somebody would like a word."

I took the phone and said, "Hello?" and I heard my mum's smile before her voice.

"Baby?" she said. "Is that you?"

"Hi, Cherry."

"Oh my *God*," she said. "I was so worried."

"Sorry."

"Don't you say sorry to me," she said. "Just promise to stay there and don't move cos we're coming to get you."

"OK, Mum, I promise."

"I missed you," she said. "Don't leave me like that again."

I stood at Sam's window looking out at the fog. His radiator was on and it was warm against my tummy. I had a bath before I went to bed, and loads to eat, and I was wearing a pair of pyjamas that must have been Sam's years and *years* ago cos they actually nearly fit me. And I could smell my clean hair and my clean clothes in the warm room and I felt happy.

And, as I looked, a car came through the fog. Its lights came first and they lit the fog up from within and it looked like a solid thing, and I could see the shadow of a tree inside it. Then the car came, yellow and old and pointy, and it turned to the left and stopped.

The doors opened and I saw them, all of them. Mum and Sam and Isabel and Doormat and Mick and Steve. They stood looking up at the house, and I ran out of my room and knocked on Sam's mum and dad's bedroom door.

I said, "He's home! They're here! Wake up!"

And we went running downstairs to meet them.

Thank yous to:

Veronique Baxter

Laura West

Stella Paskins

Gillie Russell

and Bohemia Houghton

About the author

Jenny Valentine moved house every two years when she was growing up. She worked in a wholefood shop in Primrose Hill for fifteen years where she met many extraordinary people and sold more organic loaves than there are words in her first novel, *Finding Violet Park*. She has also worked as a teaching assistant and a jewellery maker. She studied English Literature at Goldsmiths College, which almost put her off reading but not quite.

Jenny is married to a singer/songwriter and has two children. Her first novel, *Finding Violet Park*, won the Guardian Children's Fiction Prize in 2007.

"Ultra-original and brilliantly written, this will have you laughing and crying too."

Mizz Magazine

Winner of the
Guardian Children's
Fiction Prize
PAR AVION
LENTOPOSTI
FLYGPOST
Jenny Valentine
BROKEN
SOUP
Negative. Positive
It's how you look at it

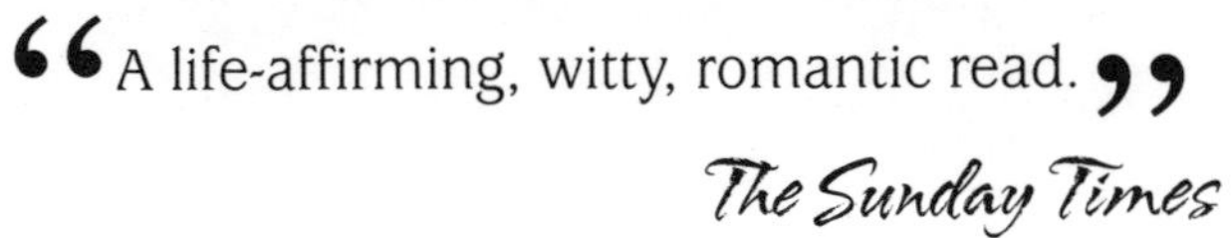
"A life-affirming, witty, romantic read."
The Sunday Times